MW01232729

she
Loved

a Life Lived
in Love

Leslie Ann Carvery

She Loved
Copyright © 2021 by Leslie Ann Carvery

All rights reserved. No part of this publication may be reproduced, distributed, or transmitted in any form or by any means, including photocopying, recording, or other electronic or mechanical methods, without the prior written permission of the author, except in the case of brief quotations embodied in critical reviews and certain other non-commercial uses permitted by copyright law.

Tellwell Talent
www.tellwell.ca

ISBN
978-0-2288-6016-7 (Hardcover)
9780-2-288-6015-0 (Paperback)
978-0-2288-6017-4 (eBook)

To all the men I have loved

Introduction

L iving a life filled with love and freedom has been the best thing I could do for myself.

Polyamory is two words, poly meaning "more than one," and "amor" meaning love. The idea is not to have lots of sex but to enjoy love.

My polyamorous journey has been filled with happiness and enlightenment. This book is a fiction to shine light on the other options a woman can embark upon in life. It is a powerful decision to leave the world of monogamy behind, and love and be loved without the restrictions and boundaries of traditional marriage. To have all the relationships you want to, simply because you have a choice and mutual consent. To engage with radical honesty in yourself and with others. To know and live by options that were not immediately presented and to leap into living, like many have never seen before or known could be possible.

The lack of drama, lies and cheating opened up my journey to love as deeply or superficially as I wanted to without painful consequences. For decades I have been flowing and dancing through love in the most organic and natural way. To be so honest in your thoughts, feelings and desires, to put sex in the place it belongs for you, seems radical in the framework of traditional love and marriage.

I don't believe poly love is for everyone any more than I believe monogamy is. But learning of one's options should be fundamental. We cannot always follow the "what always was", for we are not all the same.

In the newly opening world, I am honored to be the light in love, and to experience the upgrade of living a more intentionally designed life for myself. I was raised wonderfully, the proof is that I am alive to be the adult who now makes my own choices, does my own research and applies my learnings to my own life.

I write this romantic book of love purely to show what outside of the box love looks like. To create a thought, a conversation, and to explore the "what if". What if I were to be honest about my body, my needs, love, sex and desires, just to plant the seed?

Note: Much like love, this story moves through time and space.

Chapter 1

Montreal

Time of death

In the middle of a brisk November night, Charlene Reese took her last breath. She was lying beside her loving husband, the man she had lived and loved with for the past 20 years. Her partner, Anton Henry, cried silently. "Partner" was the New Age term they used because although their love was strong, their title was complicated. Anton might have been her partner and common-law husband in residence, but Charlene Reese had many lovers. She had managed many feelings, emotions, schedules and relationships.

Charlene drifted gently away from her beautiful life, leaving behind love, goals, achievements, adventures and friends. The romantic world she had created for herself came to an end with her final breath. Her passing was about to ignite massive streams of pain throughout her world. With her memories and thoughts scrambled and receding, there was little left for her to be present for. She just fell into a sleep forever; her legacy was about to take form. The snippets of quilt patterns would begin to unite as people spoke of her existence.

Anton Henry heard her small, shallow breathing cease sometime before the sun came up. He wrapped his arms around her last moments of warmth and waited for the light to fill the room. The dreadfulness of the day awaited him. His wife, his life had gone and left him. He was now without family and without the driving force that he loved for the past 20 years. Tears fell from his face onto her bare shoulder. He sobbed as flashes of all the moments of their life eddied around in his mind. Her tiny voice, the scent of her hair, the sounds she made settling in for a night's sleep. Now forever lost.

Those who knew Charlene assumed she would leave the world doing something adventurous or death defying. Ideas of Charlene climbing up great cold mountain tops or fighting a tsunami while trekking through foreign land or riding her bike through dangerous African terrain were very much in keeping with her lifestyle and reputation. No one would ever have guessed she would lose herself and die in her bed. Charlene's life was grand. She was a hunter of goals and pursuer of dreams. Charlene's condition was not made public. Her diagnosis of advanced Alzheimer's had been kept quiet from everyone. No one but Anton saw the disappearance of Charlene Reese. She made him promise that. She couldn't bear the idea of people seeing her in a weakened state.

Anton had known and loved this incredible woman for so long. Each day he was amazed at her passion and convictions. They had designed and made a relationship that worked. No one could ever say they saw them fight or show anything but pure adoration towards each other. Anton and Charlene were the couple that strangers wished they could be. Their loved scared the ones who knew them best. Now it was all over. Their partnership had come to an end. Death was the only thing that could separate them. With the special relationship they lived, it could only be death.

Small cries and muffled wails could be heard from the 11th floor Montreal condo. The sun had risen and Anton had pulled himself up out of the bed that still cradled his beloved. It had been the longest most dreadful night of his life. Throughout the night Anton remained on the edge of the bed where he had always slept, leaving his queen all the space to create her amazing dreams. Anton knew his wife would not make it through the night, just as he also knew she would never consider a trip to the hospital. His beloved Charley's brain was the first to shut down. Her dementia was rapidly destroying every thought and memory she had. She went from one day of being disoriented to being bedridden.

For the past few weeks Anton made her as comfortable as possible, waiting for the few tiny moments of her being his Charley again. Not the warrior of a woman he knew for the past twenty-some years, but even the soft and gentle senior who might laugh at an old memory they had shared. Anton knew that woman was locked away under so much life, yet she barely could remember her name most days. Her vacant look always sparked pain for Anton. She was the woman who loved life, the woman who challenged the world with her presence. Charlene had always been on top of her game, rarely caught without an answer, be it accurate or witty. She had charmed the world. With this joie *de vie.*

It was painful to see the absence of her. He had sheltered this version of her for the past couple of months from friends and family, knowing she would want it that way. Charlene was a proud woman. She never wanted to appear unfocused. We see that enough in the world she would say, people need positivity. Many people looked up to his wife. Her cycling fans, her art circles, she had quite a following of friends and fans of all ages and backgrounds.

Even at age seventy-one, Anton was still a fit man. He was tall, and now thinner than he was in his younger days. A serious vegetarian for most of his life, Anton was a strong Caribbean man. He was still easily able to care for himself and his wife in their small condo. Their life was simple. They had purchased the Griffintown apartment eight years ago. It was perfect for Charlene's art and projects.

Every day was routine for him. He drank a health shake and did some form of Tai Chi or Yoga daily. He ate fresh fruit and vegetables. He did the grocery shopping twice a week and cleaned the house while Charlene laid in her room forgetting bits of her wonderful life. It baffled him the way things turned out. He was always so sure she would outlive him or be his caretaker in their golden years. He never guessed this would be their reality. He didn't even have the luxury of wishing for more time. Charlene would have hated being around longer just in her body with moments of being present and moments of being lost. Twenty great years of laughter, tenderness, getting each other and comfort. It was a ride like no other, he reminded himself. It was going to be very hard staying positive without her.

The coroner and one Montreal police officer left the apartment at 12 noon. It was horribly quiet. The stillness was quite unsettling. They had taken his best friend and she would never walk through that door again. Anton sat, unable to move, watching them gently cover and remove Charlene from their home. An hour passed before Anton sat down at his desk and constructed a list of names. A list of the people who needed to hear firsthand about the death of his wife. He would need to make three calls straight away. There would be many to follow. He knew time was an issue. Knowing how quickly social media can run with information, he got straight to the job at hand. He knew doing these things would keep his emotions from taking flight.

Charlene was a popular woman. She had friends, family and fans all over the world. She had a son overseas and a mother in another Province. This news was going to devastate so many people. He first reached for his cell phone, then changed his mind and reached for Charlene's phone. His first call was to the second name on her contact list. Darrin Reese, her only child. Darrin lived in Europe; Anton didn't have the energy to check the time difference. It was one of those times when waking someone would be okay, because nothing else was.

It was early evening in Amsterdam. Darrin answered his cell phone thinking his mom was trying to reach him. It had been a while since the two had spoken. But that was Charlene Reese, she could just disappear for weeks at a time.

The bar was quite noisy, so he rushed into his office and closed the door.

"Mom," he sounded out of breath.

"It's me, son" Anton spoke softly into the phone. Anton was known for his soft heartedness. He cried easily and this time was no different. The sound of sniffles went on as Darrin waited to hear the words.

Darrin had known his mother was not doing well, even her social media posts seemed strange. But this was the last thing he expected to hear. Charlene Reese was the very image of golden aged health. She was cycling all day, every day, as soon as the Canadian winter ceased. She was mapping adventures and training.

"Wait ...She, Anton, are you saying she is gone?" Darrin raised his voice. He hoped for anything now, tell him she had a bike accident and broke a few bones, tell him she is in bed resting from a bad virus but please, he thought, don't let the words dead or passed into this call. He hoped.

Anton tried again to make his voice clear. He nodded and cried,

"Yes, she died last night in bed," he managed.

Darrin closed his eyes and said a few words he wasn't sure were even English before hanging up the phone. The call lasted less than three minutes. He just sat there absorbing his most feared loss.

One hour passed and Darrin found himself alone behind the bar. His bar had never been closed before for personal reasons. But on this horrible day, the day he found out his mother had left the world, Darrin sent all the staff and patrons home. Everyone was shocked by his sudden change. Darrin had always been the easy-going bar lord at Newman's Bar, a small cocktail lounge in the town centre. At 7:30 that evening Darrin helped staff with their coats, threw half drank pints down the drain and quickly moved the grumbling patrons towards the door. His whole personality had switched from confident, good-humoured businessman to lost kid with a sense of urgency and despair. Darrin looked broken and childlike as he pushed everyone to get their belongings.

"I will call Sara if you like," Tiffany said, pulling her coat off the top of the pile. Tiffany was one of the bar maids and best friend to his girlfriend Sara. Darrin said nothing but his body language gave way to the depths of his pain. Tiffany called her friend before leaving her emotional boss. Darrin poured a large shot from his personal whiskey decanter. In what seemed like only minutes since the staff left, a pounding on the door demanded his attention and the ringing of his cell phone made for an urgent rhythm. He opened the door to let his girlfriend Sara Jansen in with a cold gust of wind. She could feel the heavy darkness as soon as she entered. Nothing about this man resembled her boyfriend of three years. Darrin was furrowed and confused as he opened the door for her.

"What is it?" She waited until Darrin had walked back behind the bar. He fidgeted with the glass, pushing it back and forth with cupped hands. Darrin always fidgeted with things. He had compulsions to always have something moving, spinning, rotating and flicking. The more stressed he became, the more noticeable this affliction was.

"What is it? Is it your mother?" she asked with genuine concern. He couldn't find the words. He nodded, letting all his tears fall. Darrin cried for hours before announcing his need go back to Montreal. Sara nodded quickly, going through her own schedule in her head. Her passport was up to date. She and Darrin had planned on going to Canada in the following months. She had been looking forward to meeting the grand woman who gave life to the man she loved. She had heard lots about the adventures of Charlene Reese.

"I can come with you. I will book us a flight, let me just clear some things. Darrin let's just go home and make some calls, let me be there for you," She pleaded.

Darrin had no objections, he knew he needed Sara. He couldn't even think, let alone fly himself from Amsterdam to Montreal. Sara was a practical woman. She was exactly what Darrin needed to help him at this time. He had been in a relationship with Sara for three years. He enjoyed her practicality and warmth. Sara was what many referred to as a plain woman, she wore little to no makeup and hid her best features behind heavy prescription glasses. She worked hard in her field. Sara was an engineer in solar panels for agriculture. But when explaining it to his friends in Canada, Darrin teased that she made windmills. It was a joke they both enjoyed. Dutch agriculture.

The following morning, Darrin sat on the edge of his bed watching as Sara placed his clothes into his black duffel bag. He had stitched patches on it from several of his travels. The bag was covered in European and Latin American flags. "It will be cold there, how many sweaters should I pack?" She asked grabbing all his ties and tossing them into his duffel bag.

"You will need a suit," Sara went back into the closet and grabbed a garment bag.

"I have some things there. In the storage at mom's condo," he retorted.

Sara was a list-maker. On the bed she had a hand-written to-do list. Darrin looked at it and was surprised at the level of organization this woman displayed. Her mid-sized suitcase was parked at the doorway and his was already filled with almost his entire wardrobe. She closed it up and ticked off the last task on her list.

"Don't wear black," Darrin mumbled.

"What's that?" Sara struggled to lift his heavy bag off the bed.

"My mom would hate to have people wearing black at her funeral. She would hate having a funeral, come to think of it," he tried to smile.

Darrin knew his mother had no time for old traditions and doing things the way everyone else did. She was often scorned upon by the deeply religious and conservatives in her town. Many knew of her anti-establishment ways. She had been labelled an anarchist by some.

"She made Anton and I promise that there would be no religion, black-dressing or tears, those were her demands in regards to her celebration of life," Darrin's face was childlike as he spoke.

Sara unzipped her pink suitcase and reached in, grabbing her Lillian Wong designer black dress, and tossing it out onto the floor. She rezipped her luggage and rolled it towards the door.

"Okay then...Ready," she announced. Sara hugged her boyfriend. She was sure she could get them to Canada and take care of him. It made her feel good to be there for him.

Anton knew after phoning Darrin, he should call Shelly Valentine. Knowing Shelly, she would be there within the hour and offer great assistance to the rest of the calls he had to make. Shelly had been like a daughter to Charley. Shelly had lived with Anton and Charlene for a small time and the two were very close. Shelly was quite a bit younger and their friendship had been solid for decades. Charlene first met Shelly when Shelly was just a 10-year-old girl, when they both lived back in Nova Scotia. Little Shelly Valentine found herself in dance lessons paid for by her school. She was the smallest student in Charlene's dance class. Years later, Shelly moved to Montreal and had been a ray of sunshine to Charlene and Anton. It pained him to call her with this news. Shelly was one of the few people who knew Charley was sick. But she could never have guessed it was this grave.

"She's gone now. Charley is gone," was all Anton said on the phone.

"I am on my way," Shelly responded. She wanted to panic and break down, but she knew she had to get to Anton as soon as possible. Leaving a message for her husband Vern, Shelly grabbed her purse and headed out of her apartment. He would need her. Charlene was his everything.

Shelly bombarded the doors of the Griffin Street building. On most occasions, Shelly would have an exchange of pleasantries with Abdul, the door man. But on this day, he buzzed her through the front door, barley making eye contact. Abdul liked his tenants' little friend, Shelly, with the small body and huge smile, but he didn't have words for anyone after seeing the ambulance cart away Charlene Reese. Abdul failed to make eye contact as Shelly moved with purpose through the entrance and onto the elevator. She could feel the sting of tears and pain as she neared the door. Shelly had a key to apartment 1110, she often knocked and then let herself in. She did so slowly and gently.

Anton was sitting in Charley's art nook. Charlene's finished paintings were leaning against all the walls. The smell of oil paint lingered in the small area. Her newest unfinished painting was still wet on the easel. Charlene had been painting daily for the past 15 years after retiring her career in dance. Every painting showed more skill and patience. She had really come into her expression as an artist. She would paint for hours. Many paintings were sold through an online gallery. Many she gave away as gifts.

Shelly had never seen Anton so withdrawn. He had always been such a big presence since the day they first met. He was a well-built man with an infectious laugh. The sound of Charlene and Anton laughing was a constant in that household. Anton enjoyed Charlene's wacky sense of humour. They lived for witty comments and inside jokes. Never had the apartment been so quiet and hollow. Shelly reached in and hugged him around his belly button. He was a giant to her, but on this occasion, he was small and frail.

"I will make us a pot of tea," Shelly said as she headed for the kitchen. That was always the first thing Charlene did when anyone visited. She put on a pot of tea.

After pouring two steamy cups of tea, Shelly had Anton seated in the living room. His long body falling back on the small sofa. The life had been knocked from him.

"Did you call Darrin?" Shelly asked, placing the tray in front of them.

Anton nodded. He didn't reach for his cup. He sat there looking at it, afraid to look anywhere else in the room.

"He will be here tomorrow, he is coming with Sara," he said. His voice was gentle and filled with emotion. Shelly nodded and sipped from her favourite mug. She had bought the set for Charlene years ago.

She perked up for a second.

"Great! We finally get to meet Sara!"

But instantly, the sadness hit her that Charlene had been so looking forward to meeting her son's love. She had seen a few pictures and was desperate to find out what Darrin liked about this seemingly plain woman.

"What about the others? Her mom and the guys?" she asked.

Anton pointed in the direction of his desk. On top of many papers and books was a list. Shelly read it through. She had known or heard of every one of these people throughout the years of her friendship with Charlene. Charlene Reese had so many types of relationships. These were the people closest to her heart. Her lovers.

The list named six men and their phone numbers, all written out in Anton's perfect handwriting.

"You made a list. Did you contact any of them?" her voice was gentle.

Anton shook his head and reached for his cup. "Charley had made the list before...I only contacted Cora, her mom. I thought I would wait for you before notifying the others," he said.

"How did Cora take it?" Shelly asked.

Shelly had met Charlene's mother a few times. She knew Charlene was Cora's last living offspring.

"She couldn't say much. She cried and said she would call me later," Anton said with tears filling his eyes.

"It must have been heart-breaking to inform her mother," Shelly stifled her own tears. Anton nodded.

Shelly sat there trying to hold everything in. They had a long day ahead of them. She brought the list back to her seat. "We should start," she insisted. The list felt heavy in her little hand. This was not an everyday death announcement. After all, who can say they had to call six lovers after the death of a senior aged woman? Charlene, in life or death, never followed the path of average.

Chapter 2

The Calls

The name Ash Adams appeared first on Anton's list. Anton had never met Ash before, but Shelly remembered a few stories about him.

"He is the race car driver from the States. Charlene has told me many stories about him. He is the one who took her to Greece, but they didn't spend a lot of time together," Shelly informed as she waved the list in her fingers.

"I got this one," Shelly said, and started punching in his phone number. When she did this, a photo of him showed on the screen of Charlene's phone. Ash was a husky and handsome man. A golden-brown complexion. His face looked kind as he smiled for the picture. Shelly took a deep breath before pressing the green phone symbol. His line rang one time before he answered. Shelly was nervous and hoped her voice would work.

Ash's voice was gentle and happy sounding when he answered. He thought he was about to have a conversation with a woman he adored. Shelly released the breath and said his name.

"Ash, is this Mr. Ash Adams?" the strange woman asked.

The whole time Shelly spoke this horrible news, Ash tried to remember the last conversation he had with Charlene. It had been quite some time since he had seen her. He received a gift in the mail from her a few years back, but it had been at least five years since he had his big arms around her. After Shelly broke the regrettable news, Ash hung the phone up and took a seat on his bed. The memories of his special friend flooded his head. She was the most alive person he had ever met. He was surprised that such a healthy and determined woman could be gone, just like that. He thought of her as a young woman in all their moments together. He remembered her dancing on the beach in Mykonos Island. They had not spent a great deal of time together, just stolen moments over a long period of time. Ash Adams remembered the day he met Charlene. He had to take a bus to Texas for a race. He was being presented with a brand-new PT Cruiser as a gift from the promoters, so he bought a one-way bus ticket. Ash was fast in the car but slow in life, so he was the last one to board the bus. There were a few seats available and he selected one next to the prettiest passenger.

She was a red-boned girl with a tight little frame. He saw the other woman give him eyes as he moved toward her empty seat.

"Is this seat taken?" he asked, hoping it wasn't. The pretty passenger looked up and gave her approval, she removed her bag from the vacant chair and waved him in. Ash whistled out his southern charm and she enjoyed his attention. That weekend he won the race, got a new car and spent two days entertaining the most beautiful and exciting woman he had ever met. They kept in touch and had a few more exciting rendezvous over the years. After a failed marriage, Ash kept his bachelor card. He liked the single life and its perks. One of those perks was Charlene Reese.

Ash had lived in Charlotte, North Carolina all his life. At 67 years old, he lived a quiet life in the basement apartment of his daughter Helen's house. She was divorced with two grown sons. They all lived just outside the city. Ash used to take long walks with the oldest boy Kevin, but both boys were away at college and the house was very quiet those days.

Helen made her nightly visits to check on her father after work. She would normally bring him something she cooked or an occasional treat from the bakery. After entering the house and putting her shopping away Helen made her way down the basement steps towards her dad's place. She knocked lightly on his door while kicking her laundry further into the laundry room. She closed the door to the laundry room while waiting on her father to open his door. She was about to leave, guessing he might be out when she heard sounds.

"Dad? Are you in there?" Helen has always given her father his space and privacy, but that sound was so unfamiliar and unnerving, she quickly made a decision. Reaching for the key she had hidden under the dryer, Helen opened the door and rushed into her father's apartment. She was shocked to find him on the floor, just lying there crying.

"Dad? Dad, what is it? Dad you're scaring me," Helen sat on the floor and held her dad.

Ash continued to weep as his daughter helped him onto his bed and made him his favourite hot cocoa. He insisted on real milk, not that stupid almond stuff Helen used.

"Do you want to talk about it?" Asked Helen. She was concerned. She rarely saw her father in such a state. He had always been a calm and fun type of man. He drank rarely and loved his hobbies and friends. Ash Adams was a race car driver back in his day. He married young and divorced after ten years. He never remarried. He often went on drives to Louisiana to visit with some of his race car friends. He was not in any way a lonely man, and he still had a good look about him that attracted all the old girls. Helen was baffled by his sudden mood change.

"Should I call a doctor?" she asked, not knowing what to do next.

Ash didn't exactly know why, but he wasn't ready to talk about Charlene with his daughter. She wouldn't understand, he figured.

"I'll be alright, I just got some news...it was upsetting is all," he managed to say.

"Was it one of your friends? Did one of your racing friends die?" She asked.

That sounded like a fair guess. Ash nodded. He was only being deceitful because he really didn't want to talk about any of this yet.

"Oh dad, I am so sorry. If you want, I can have one of the boys take you to Louisiana to pay respects. Kevin is coming home this weekend, that should cheer you up."

Ash nodded, hoping that would be enough to get his daughter out of his room and leave him with the thoughts consuming his head. His beautiful memories of their special times danced in his thoughts.

Ash was so thoroughly distracted that he didn't notice when Helen left. The door was shut and relocked again. He got up and went to his closet. He pulled out boxes and envelopes, the closet was packed with his life. Many trophies and place ribbons, car magazines and model cars he had built with his grandkids. There was so much all packed into his closet. "Where did I put the box?" he asked out loud. After a long search, Ash found his shoe box of small mementos. He placed the box on the table and drank his cocoa. He had received a gift from Charlene years ago. It was there in the box. He had never pulled it out of its case. He had received it in the mail so long ago. Ash felt heavy sitting at his table looking at the handwriting on the box. The writing of a woman he promised to love forever.

Montreal

Years Before:

Anton found Charlene deeply immersed in creative activity when he came home from the gym. She had her craft box out and that focused look in her eyes.

Making his protein shake, he watched her move around the apartment plugging in her glue gun, leaving trails of glitter everywhere.

Anton was curious enough to wonder out loud, "May I ask what you're working on?" He was always amused by her strong, creative passion. When an idea hit Charlene, she would be off and running with it.

Charlene shook her head, indicating she wasn't ready to share yet. These little gestures were commonplace when she found herself immersed in a project. Charlene could zone out the world to focus on one thing. She enjoyed her projects and energy.

A few hours later, Charlene entered the bedroom, where Anton was watching his favourite TV show. He muted the TV to give her his attention.

"I have a gift for you," she smiled

"For me?" Anton was surprised.

"Well not just for you, for...the guys," She climbed onto the bed, still holding his present in her hand.

She then began to explain something she had come across online. Charlene was very much into social media. She spent a lot of her day on the computer interacting with people and promoting her art.

"I read this article about Lenny Kravitz, Lisa Bonet and Jason Momoa all sharing a designated piece of jewellery to show unity. They were not polyamorous but still a step ahead of normal monogamous traditions. I thought it was an amazing gesture and I wanted to do something similar to honour the love ones with whom I have shared myself" she smiled like a little girl with a secret.

Anton nodded, knowing how giving and caring his lover could be.

"But I cannot afford jewellery since, well you know, I am poor," she laughed.

"So, I made these," she beamed.

With Glitter glue stuck to her fingers, she slowly opened her palm and dropped the small gift in Antón's large brown hand. It was a shot glass with the word "Love" hand-written in glitter.

"Beautiful," he smiled.

"Thank you," she was proud of her creative treasure.

With that, Charlene jumped off the bed and started the shipping process for her little gift giving adventure. She found small packing boxes and started addressing them to her dearests.

Anton also decided to use Charlene's phone for the next call. Shelly passed it to him as she went to heat more water for tea. The number was found in her contacts under Tennessee James Parker. The funny thing was, Charlene also called him Tennessee James. For many years Anton assumed that was really his name until she revealed there were many men in her life named James. Local James, Jersey, James, James the Asian cyclist, and Tennessee James. It was just practical. But it was Tennessee James she had special feelings for.

The time zone difference had James Parker still drinking his morning coffee when a call from Charlene Reese's number buzzed his phone. He became excited with the anticipation of hearing her voice. He and Charlene had not spoken in a while, but a huge smile lit up his face upon seeing her name on his phone display. "Morning Reesy, to what do I owe this pleasure?" his voice was smooth with a soothing bass tone to it.

"Is this James Parker?" Anton asked.

James knew before this man spoke again exactly what the call was for. When you reach a certain age, these conversations become unfortunately common.

"James, this is Anton Henry, Charlene's partner," Anton kept his tone low.

"Yeah," was all James could manage.

"Sorry to have to make this call, brother," Anton continued. "I called to inform you that Charlene Reese has passed away. She had struggled with an aggressive form of Alzheimer's and she died this morning. I know the two of you were…close."

James could not believe the words. He had never met Anton but had heard through his Reesy what a great man he was.

Not familiar with how any of this works, James was at a loss for words.

"She died in her sleep?" was all James could say.

Anton confirmed, and said that she was at peace.

James knew Reesy was never a Religious type, and in life or death, you couldn't get that woman in a church.

"Will there be a…any kind of…service?" he inquired.

Anton almost let a small smirk escape. "I will notify you once we settle on the best kind of farewell celebration," Anton said.

"I understand, I...uh thank you," James disconnected the call and sat down.

"Oh Reesy," sighed James. Placing his phone on the kitchen table, he poured himself another coffee.

Nashville

An hour had passed, and James remained at the table lost in thought. He didn't hear his ex-wife let herself in. James divorced Marcy over six years ago, but every day she dropped by, did his laundry, cleaned his kitchen and made him a meal. Marcy greeted James with a cheerful hello and then started unpacking groceries. She often hummed an old hymn as she did housework.

"The market was busy today, I don't know if I want to continue to go to that store anymore, not one cashier, no one greets you or helps you. I don't like the way people do business these days."

James smiled, having heard the same conversation from Marcy for years. Marcy was a simple and easy woman. She lived for days gone by and complained constantly about things she couldn't change.

"I am going to make you up some fish and beans, then I got to leave early today. You know Mrs. Little from the church? Her son was killed in Houston. We are having a little thing down at the parish, you wanna come?" she asked knowing very well what her ex-husbands response would be.

James shook his head, "You ain't never seen my ass in a church since I married you," he teased.

"I should have known then you were the devil," she laughed loudly.

"Ain't gotta be the devil to be a non-believer," James fought back.

Marcy hated when James spoke like that. She tried everything to bring him to God, but he just seemed to be constantly drifting in the opposite direction. He always had to be difficult.

"I don't know who fills your head with such things," she always said. The closest she ever got to an answer was, "I met a free woman once, she told me things."

"I am bringing your clothes over to my place to wash them, save some time. Besides, your dryer is doing that thing again, taking twice as long to dry the towels," she huffed.

"I am gonna need my clothes ...I will do my own wash," James jumped up and said.

"You?" Marcy stopped what she was doing and looked at her ex-husband. "Why would you do your clothes?" she inquired. She knew something was wrong. James seemed off, more distant than usual.

"I have to go somewhere. I am taking a trip," he announced. Just as much to her as himself.

Marcy just stood there looking at this old fool in front of her. He never went anywhere these days. He said he had too much of traveling before he retired.

"Yeah okay, I will have them back first thing tomorrow," she promised. "I'll pack your suitcase too if ya like," she added. Marcy was out the door with his clothes before he could say any more about it. James never asked Marcy to do all the things she did for him, but he also never asked her not to. Soon, James was left to his thoughts again. Reesy and Marcy were the two most important women in his life. He married Marcy because he loved her and ran from Reesy because she scared him. Her freeness, her ability to not care about the masses, it was all too much for him.

Montreal

Shelly just sat there knowing she had to make the next call. She could feel a chill in the room, found a window cracked open and shut it.

"Did you know Tennessee James? "she asked Anton, returning to her seat.

"No, never met him. She told me lots about him, he used to whisk her away on trips and then he got married. They changed their relationship for a while. They played some game online together; I can't remember what. But she would laugh like a child when she was winning." he mused

Shelly smiled "I remember, they went to Vegas and the Grand Canyon. He's the guy who used to write her poetry," Shelly added.

"I think you're right. They didn't continue a deep relationship after we got together. He didn't understand any of it. She was hurt, but they continued as friends," Anton recalled.

Shelly held the phone and thought about it. She knew Charlene had such a way with men, it never occurred to her that someone would reject her love.

Anton nodded and returned to the list. The next name was Michael Sylva, another American man. Shelly made the call.

"Hello there," Shelly took a deep breath. "Mr. Payne, this is Shelly Valentine, a friend of Charlene Reese's,"

"Oh, Lena, is Lena okay?" his voice filled with concern. Shelly could tell this man was much older than the others. His voice was small and almost inaudible.

"I am sorry Mr. Sylva, I am calling you to tell you that Charlene passed away last night. She had been sick lately." Shelly waited for the caller to respond.

"Hello" she repeated

"Yes, I am here, I just…and who are you? "he asked

'I am Shelly Valentine, a close friend of Charlene's," she repeated.

"Oh yes, right, So Lena, has passed on? She is still young and full of life, are you sure you have the right person, Charlene Reese?" He looked around the apartment while speaking to this lady.

"Mr. Sylva, I know this is upsetting news, Charlene had mentioned you often, I know you were good friends for many years," Shelly continued.

"Yes, yes, we were, Lena was my muse, she used to model my clothing line. Did she get my last package? I sent her some things, oh, about a month ago now, she always liked the things I sent her you know, she looked really beautiful in…red, she looked amazing in red. I think I have a red dress in one of these boxes," Michael continued rambling on while he opened a couple of the boxes stacked in his living room.

"Mr. Sylva, I am going to send you information soon regarding any life celebration plans," Shelly said.

It didn't seem like Michael Sylva was paying much attention to Shelly before she disconnected the call.

"Poor old guy," she said to Anton.

The anguished tears from others seemed to be taking a toll on Shelly's own pain.

"Michael Sylvia," She said after hanging up.

Anton nodded. "He is an older gentleman, the fella who sent Charley all those clothes."

"Ahh yeah, I remember. She would get these packages in the mail, and if they didn't fit, she would pass them to me," Shelly said fondly.

Shelly recalled being with Charlene when one of those packages arrived. She opened it like a child on Christmas. He had sent her stockings, leggings and a sexy animal print top. It was hard not to be envious of Charlene and her many admirers.

Shelly knew Anton didn't want to make any more calls. He leaned back in the chair trying not to cry again. She checked the list and searched for the next contact. It had begun to rain, and Anton went over to his record collection and selected an album. Soft Jazz filled the room. He turned the volume down and beckoned Shelly to continue.

Derrick Benton's phone had been disconnected. The name Shirley Hinner had been listed on Charlene's phone. The history showed Charlene had texted and called this number a few times. Shelly looked up the code and found it was located in the Bahamas. She placed her call to Nassau.

Shelly had not heard of Derrick or Shirley before, but her interest was piqued at the thought of Derrick having transitioned into a woman. Now that would be an interesting turn of events. She almost laughed as the phone connected to Shirley Matherson.

A song of a voice answered the phone. "Hello," she gave no name or didn't seem to recognize where the call was from

"Shirley? Shelly asked

"Yes, it is I," her Island accent was thick.

"Hi this is Shelly Valentine, I am calling from Montreal. I was looking for Derrick Reid"

Shirley took a very deep breath before responding.

"I am sorry, but my husband Derrick passed away about three years ago," she replied curtly.

Unprepared for that, Shelly just sat there in the dead silence, not sure how to go forward.

"Hello?" Shirley finally attempted to continue the conversation.

'I'm sorry, I am actually calling to let him know of the passing of a friend," Shelly answered carefully.

Shirley was quiet this time. "So sad, and who was this friend?" she inquired.

"Her name was Charlene Reese," Shelly informed her.

Shelly could hear the breath leave Shirley's mouth.

"Are you saying Charlene Reese just died?" Shirley's voice regained its power.

"Yes," Shelly confirmed.

Shirley nodded to the phone, "Well, please send my condolences to the family. Thank you for calling." Shirley disconnected the call and thought about the words. The death of Charlene Reese. A woman she only met briefly but will always remember. She dialled up her best friend Dory Layne. She had never spoken about Charlene to Dory, but she really wanted to talk about her now.

Back in Montreal, the next call was not going to be easy for either of them.

"It's Pierre" Shelly informed Anton. This was the one call Shelly couldn't bear to make. Pierre was too close. He lived in Montreal and they had all spent so much time together.

"I got this," Anton sat up. He used his own phone. He and Pierre had been friends for many years. This was going to be a painful conversation. Pierre and Charlene spent so much time together. Anton knew this was going to break him in many ways.

Pierre's answering service kicked in. Anton hung up and put the phone down on the table. Before Shelly could speak, the phone rang and Anton picked it up, speaking in French.

"Bonjour Pierre," Anton began.

"I am afraid I have very bad news Pierre."

Pierre knew Charlene had been getting worse, but he stayed away, knowing she was recently agitated when he visited.

"She is getting worse. I will come over, I can leave now…" Pierre's voice was full of concern and fear.

"No, she…I am so sorry…" Anton reached for the box of tissues. Shelly left the room.

"Did, is she…"

Anton could not tell if Pierre was searching for an English word or if he has succumbed to his emotions.

"She died this morning," Anton said.

The call was short. Anton ended it with, "Je suis desole, I am sorry." He promised more information to follow.

That call took a lot out of Anton. He covered his face with his large brown hands. Shelly held back her own tears. Pierre was bound to be in pieces, they both certainly knew.

Pierre placed his phone on the table and sat in his chair by the window. How could his Cheri be gone? She was fine a month before. They had taken a little trip up to northern Quebec in September. She wanted to show him some of her biking trails. Pierre had rented a cabin for the weekend and they enjoyed their short vacation. How could she be gone? Pierre let the tears burn down his cheeks and drop onto his shirt. He shook his head in disbelief. He wasn't sure what to do now. His beloved Cheri had left him forever. The pain was too much.

"The last name on the list," Shelly said, reaching for the phone. These phone calls were the most painful calls she had ever had to make, telling the men who loved Charlene most that the woman they admired for so long was gone from their lives forever.

Anton didn't need to look at the list, he knew that the last name belonged to Marlon Styles, the famous singer from Toronto.

Marlon Styles had a great showbiz career that lasted decades, but currently, he was far from being on top. Recent reports had Marlon living on the street and battling a drug addiction. Anton hoped this rumour wasn't true.

"She used to tell me all the stories about their love affair," Shelly said, as she started preparing a plate of fruit and veggies for them to share.

"Yeah, he was one of her greatest loves. They were together when we met," he said knowing Shelly had heard the story many times.

"Yeah, she would get that little sparkle in her eyes when she spoke of Marlon, they loved each other for a long time," Shelly said sadly.

Anton threw a couple of dates and walnuts on the plate Shelly had beautifully prepared for them.

"Yeah, she said they met when she was 19 years old. Can you imagine an ongoing love for that length of time? I get it, she was so...intoxicating. I would never have let her go," Anton declared.

"You did let her go. I mean, you let her be free," Shelly smiled warmly.

Anton carried the plate to his spot and put it down between them.

"She was free when I met her. Every man who ever loved her loved that about her." Anton smiled when he spoke of his lady.

"You both were my relationship goals in my life. I only ever wanted to be free like Charlene and accepting like you. I would have never believed such a relationship could work until I met you. I am so glad I had her in my life all these years," Shelly proclaimed.

"She thought of you as her daughter, you know that?" He smiled.

"She was mother, big sister, best friend and ride or die chick to me," Shelly grinned.

There was no phone number for Marlon listed in Charlene's contacts. Anton said he would leave word with him on his social media messenger. He had met Marlon once. Anton knew this day was going to shake the world of people in his partner's circles. He also knew it was going to shake Marlon Styles the most.

Shelly reclined on the sofa and nestled into Anton. She didn't want to leave him. A few calls to work and her husband had her cleared to camp out with her dear friend Anton for the night. She had always loved coming to visit their place, seeing the new paintings Charlene was working on, hearing the stories of her adventures, watching her and Anton laughing at the constant inside jokes they shared.

Both Anton and Shelly fell asleep on the sofa and were awakened by the early eastern sun streaming through the window. Shelly stretched her small frame and slowly pulled herself up.

"I can't believe you slept here too, weren't you uncomfortable?" she asked him

Anton unfolded his long body and jumped up. "I would not be more uncomfortable getting into the bed my wife just...."

Shelly jumped up and wrapped her short arms around him.

"I am so sorry," she whispered, holding back the urge to cry.

"I am so sorry," she repeated. Anton was a gentle man. He was big in size but soft all over. He was known to cry openly. Shelly knew what her job was for the next few days. Charlene would have insisted she take care of Anton and help him unpack his baggage of sorrow and grief. This was going to be quite a task. Anton was an empath and regular outside troubles burrowed into his soul.

"Let me make some tea, I will run across the street and grab a few croissants from Fred's bakery," she insisted. Anton nodded his agreement. Shelly was up and moving quickly. Anton put away the blanket he had used to cover them. When Shelly left the apartment, he half expected his beloved to come out of the bedroom with her wild bed hair, wearing her favourite night shirt with penguins on icebergs. She would walk through the apartment for minutes not talking, then just suddenly blurt out something funny and random. The place seemed overly quiet.

Shelly returned quickly. The tea and pastries smelled delicious as they both got back to the work at hand.

"So now that her mother, son, and lovers have been informed, we really need to put it out on social media before others do," proposed Shelly.

"Yes, I have been writing out a statement. It's on my tablet. If you like it, just post it." Anton went to the bathroom for a shower. Shelly clicked on his Facebook and read his announcement. He wrote it on her page.

"It is with great sadness that I tell the friends and family of Charlene Reese, that as of yesterday morning Charlene died peacefully in her sleep. Charlene had battled with dementia for the past six months and has left the world she

knew and loved at age 65. Charlene will be greatly missed. Information will follow on her celebration of life ceremony. Anton Henry'

Shelly clicked to post the message and it was instantaneous how the tablet came alive with bells and bleeps from that moment on. The whole apartment was buzzing, cell phones and computers started beeping with notifications. People were waking to the sad news. Anton returned from the bathroom. "So, it begins," he stated calmly.

Chapter 3

The Flights

Darrin rested his head on Sara's shoulder during takeoff. Her long brown hair smelled of lilacs and made him feel comforted. Once the plane lifted off the ground, he squeezed her hand. He had so many feelings and emotions rushing through his body. He fidgeted with his pen, rolling it between his fingers.

"Whenever my mom and I travelled together, she always fell asleep on ascent. Soon as the plane hit speed on runway, she would close her eyes and then fall into this quiet sleep until the hospitality cart was three rows away. She always just magically woke up in time to ask for a tea with milk." He smiled at the memory. Travels with his mom were the best of times.

"You both travelled a lot together," Sara observed. She had heard already about a few mother-son adventures, and if you went deep into his social media photos, there were some pictures of the two of them being adventurous all over the world.

"Mhmm... The United States, Mexico, Morocco, Barcelona, Thailand, Greece...yeah, she gave me the love for travel way back when I was small. She always told me how when I was three years old, I had my own passport and suitcase and knew all the airport protocol. I had my shoes off before the security guy came over, had all my stamps on my passport. Yeah, we loved to be in the world. When I moved to Amsterdam, she came three times to visit. But she was getting older and I knew it was getting harder on her to do International travel. She's been everywhere, she knows so many people," he bragged with a gentle smile.

Sara watched her man as his happy memories flooded his handsome face. Darrin was mixed-race but he could pass for any race. Sara was shocked when he told her he was half Black and half Mexican. She had assumed his mother was the Mexican when she glimpsed a photo. Charlene was a beautiful fair skinned woman. She had many looks in her photos: long hair, curly hair, grey eyes, braids and blond tresses. But no matter the disguise of fashion, she and Darrin greatly favoured each other.

"You would have loved her, everyone did," he smiled. "She would have loved you, too," he concluded.

His mother was a Black woman from Nova Scotia. Darrin would often tell Sara stories of growing up in the Black communities of Canada. Even after hearing these stories over the past three years she had never considered Darrin's true background or about where Darrin really came from. He just seemed so at home in Europe with friends from many Countries. And now his most personal beginnings were about to be revealed. She knew during the next few days that she would learn the answers to every question she ever had about Darrin. The hidden world of his past was about to open up before her. Sara knew Darrin was an only child, but he did say he came from a big family.

Sara smiled, was about to ask him a question, and saw he had fallen asleep. The airline hostess placed a plastic cup of orange juice on Sara's tray quietly so as not to wake her sleeping companion. Sara removed the pen from his hand and placed it on her lowered tray table. She knew Darrin would need the rest. He had been spinning since the news of his mother's death came.

Marrakesh

Many Years Before

Charlene had booked the holiday for them to spend time together. Darrin was living in Barcelona at the time, attending a bartending course. The Inn was the perfect picture from a travel magazine. Darrin couldn't believe his eyes when he and Charlene entered through the huge door. They had been through chaos between the airport, harsh customs, getting a taxi and then traversing the African caves to find their lodging. Many of the locals offered help and then demanded money. Charlene became flustered, making her way through the dry heat and dusty paths. Every door looked somewhat the same, with numbers and sometimes Arabic writing. They knocked loudly at a huge door that neither believed could be their hotel. Nothing on the outside suggested what Charlene had booked online. When the huge door opened and the hotelier invited them in, both Darrin and Charlene were pleasantly surprised. The concierge had them wait in a huge atrium with natural plants and birds flying from the small trees. He brought over two shot glasses of mint tea before checking them in. A few minutes later they were being escorted up to the top floor where the pool and lounge area was. Darrin and Charlene had the only rooms on the level. It was a paradise. This is going to be my best birthday ever, *Darrin thought.*

After a quick dip in the pool, Darrin found his mother on a huge bed with pillows. She was laying down reading a book and sipping on some sweet mint tea the waiter had brought to her.

"Let me know when you are ready to go back out into the jungle and explore," Darrin said, pouring himself a small shot glass of tea.

"I think we should just stay right here for today and take on the crazy tomorrow," Charlene said, as she removed her sunglasses and stretched out under the intense African sun.

Darrin smiled. His mother was always up for an adventure. He saw how relaxed and comfortable she was, not wearing her normal alerted and high instinct travel face.

"Sounds good to me," he said, and sipped his drink.

Toronto

Cora Reese opened the door to let her older-by-one-year brother Aaron in. Cora and Aaron had moved into the same senior's residence a few years ago. Arron was on the third floor with his Jack Russel, Petey, and Cora took a well-decorated unit on the second floor. They had made a ritual of sharing eggs, tea and toast for breakfast every morning. The siblings were like an old married couple.

"I didn't think you would have breakfast today," Aaron said, moving his 91-year-old body slowly toward the table. His seat was well worn in, just the way he liked it. The scrambled eggs, all soft and yellow, were laid out on Cora's favourite decorative plate. Cora loved pretty things. She prided herself on the art of beautiful presentation.

"I didn't even know I was making breakfast. My body just started moving the way it always does," she responded.

Cora was always an attractive woman. She got up every day to make her face and dressed as if she had plans. On this day, she was still in her house coat when Aaron arrived.

Aaron started dishing up his plate. He added a few teaspoons of sugar to his tea and waited for his sister to speak. Cora was always the talkative one. Aaron often teased that the breakfast was worth the outpouring of conversation Cora always provided. But now he watched his sister sit in front of an empty plate that she hadn't even put a piece of toast on yet.

"I can't eat," she blurted.

Cora pushed the rest of the eggs toward her brother. Not wanting to be insensitive, he didn't take her offer for seconds. It was heartbreaking to see Cora lose her last remaining child. The first time she lost a child, it was Holly, so many years ago. Holly died in Ottawa three weeks after getting out of jail. She was killed, and her murderer was never found or brought to justice. Cora's eldest child died many years later at age 52, after being hit by a transport truck driving on the busy Toronto highway late one night. Now her baby girl, Charlene, died naturally in her sleep at home with her husband. There was the tiniest relief in that.

Cora just sat there silently with her brother. Their usual conversation was absent, and the silence was unsettling. Aaron finished his eggs and stood up slowly. 'I can go to Montreal with you," he offered.

Cora wanted her brother beside her, but secretly hoped one of his kids could come, too. His oldest son, Fin, was always a big help. They were both so advanced in age she knew it was not going to be easy to travel with her brother and his horrible need to smoke every few minutes. "We need Fin to make us arrangements," Cora declared shakily.

Aaron nodded. "I will call him now," he replied. Aaron looked over at his sister. She looked as though this was going to be the last upset of her life.

Toronto

Many years earlier

The memory of their worst fight remained etched in Cora's mind. She couldn't remember where she went a day ago, but she could remember every detail about her argument with her rebellious youngest daughter.

"You can't just do whatever you want in this world, Charlene Adele Reese," Cora shouted louder than she wanted to.

Charlene knew this fight with her mother had been pending for some time. The moment Cora used her full name, it was on.

"Why? Why not? Why can't I have everything I want in life and do everything I want?" Charlene spoke calmly hoping her mother would follow suit. They were finishing breakfast in her mom's place and Uncle Aaron had just left for his after-breakfast nap.

"Why do you always have to go against everything and shit on everyone's lives? People have been living a good long time before you came into this world, Charlene, and you just think you can live your life without rules and order. You are so fucking selfish," Cora spat. Cora was raging mad when she started swearing. Charlene was less mad and more amused at her flailing mother.

"Why am I selfish mom? Because I don't want to live in the hard bed I made. No. I don't want to suck it up and have a man forever and hope for a few happy moments in a lifetime of marriage. How did that work for your three marriages followed by a lifetime of being alone?" Charlene's words were sharp.

The intensity stung Cora. Her bronzed complexion flushed with anger.

"I have lived my life with dignity, thank you very much. When I die, I will have my conscience clear," Cora concluded. Her words were losing volume.

"Really, are you sure about that?" Charlene asked.

Near to tears, Cora tossed the breakfast plates into the sink and ran water over them.

"Mom, I am not going to fight with you. I am not going to change my life. I quite like it. I have two beautiful men who love me and I love them and if another one comes along, that is ok too. I am not going to do some version of old-school relationship struggles just because that is how things are done, or

that is the Christian way. You knew a long time ago I don't share this faith or commitment to follow."

"And that is why you are going to hell," Cora said before slamming the frying pan down and leaving the kitchen.

Montreal

Darrin rushed Sara out of the airport and into the cold, bitter winds of Montreal. They jumped in a cab as Darrin tried to recall the few French words he had learned from previous visits.

"Bonjourne," he greeted, and gave the driver the address to his mom's condo. Darrin relaxed in the back seat holding on to Sara's hand.

"There is...something you should know about my mom before we get to her place," Darrin began.

Sara turned to give him her full attention.

"She was a different kind of woman...a different kind of mom, really. She was...well, she..." Darrin took a deep breath, not sure how to exactly capture the lifestyle of Charlene Reese with his words. He tried again.

"My mother practised a....she lived a polyamorous lifestyle. You will meet Anton, her...husband, but just so you know, there will be others also, other...men," he mumbled.

Sara stared at Darrin for a long time.

"She was like...what, a swinger?" Sara's accent made the statement sound much worse than intended. Her words made the taxi driver laugh, which he attempted to cover up with a cough.

"No, they are not swingers. They just are not monogamous. They don't swap with other married couples. They have agreed they are both allowed to, well, date and have relationships outside of their marriage," he attempted to explain.

Sara nodded, pretending to understand. She was familiar with the word polyamorous, but she seemed to struggle with the full idea of it. Before she could ask anything else, they were pulling up into the driveway of a high rise.

Shelly waited in the lobby for Darrin and Sara's taxi to arrive. Abdul had been unusually quiet as he watched Shelly pace the lobby floor. A few tenants had entered, greeting Abdul in French and giving smiles to the little brown woman who was anxiously waiting. The taxi driver pulled up to the high rise at 11 a.m. Darrin and Sara rushed out of the car and into the nippy Montreal morning air. Abdul rushed to get the door for the luggage-toting guests.

Sara had obviously underestimated the harsh Montreal winter. Her jacket was not going to do much against -7°C with wind chill. She was pretty, Shelly thought, in a natural, girl-next-door kind of way. For sure Darrin's type, a brainy European.

They both blew through the glass doors with a gust. Darrin greeted Abdul with his limited French. Shelly hugged Darrin for a long time, then embraced Sara with family warmth. Sara stood about a whole foot taller than Shelly. She instantly wished she had not worn her heels.

"I am Shelly Valentine, a good friend of Charlene's," she introduced herself as they waited for an elevator."

"My sister from a different mister." Darrin leaned down to wrap his arm around her. Shelly was only five feet tall. The only time she had been taller than Darrin was when they first met. He was seven and she was ten.

Charlene had always teased them about being siblings due to her maternal feelings towards Shelly.

"Shelly was one of mom's dance students when we were kids," he explained to Sara.

"Yes, when this little studio rat used to roll around the place in his rollerblades," Shelly teased.

"Not much has changed," Sara said, her accent sticking to the words.

"You still skate?" Shelly asked, Pushing the 11th button on the elevator.

"Yup, I skate all over Amsterdam, it's a good workout," he laughed. "Plus, I got tired of people stealing my bikes," he admitted, and Sara confirmed with a nod.

"Everyone knows him as the roller-skating bartender," Sara added, following Shelly and Darrin down the hallway from the elevator.

Anton was waiting in the open doorway and pulled Darrin into a manly embrace. He also gave Sara a warm, welcoming hug. Darrin introduced his girlfriend to Anton. They unburdened their baggage in the hall.

"My step-friend," Anton teased

Darrin had coined the term many years ago. He knew he was past the stepdad stage, as his mom and Anton met when he was already 20 years old. So Darrin often called Anton his step-friend.

Anton stood six feet tall, having shrunk two inches since the time Darrin first met him. They were almost the same height now. Darrin was surprised at how thin Anton looked. The giant of a man looked normal in size. His long dreads were now sparse and all grey. Even Shelly had put some pounds on her small frame. *Everyone is getting older except my mom now*, he thought to himself. Charlene was always a young-hearted woman.

Sara was born and raised in the Netherlands, and although she had met many African men in Darrin's bar, she had never been this close to such a cultural difference. Everyone hugged and treated you like family. They were louder in a joyful manner. She never thought of Darrin as a Black man. She knew he was a mixed race of Black and Mexican decent, yet somehow, she didn't see him as part of this colourful dynamic. Even when African or Caribbean men came to the bar, Darrin always acted the same, never pushing his Blackness forward. You never would know his ethnicity unless you asked.

Shelly made tea and they all sat in the living room. The room was filled with colourful paintings, big pillows and painted trinkets. Sara was surprised to see an old-fashioned bean bag chair. She wanted to sit there but Darrin rushed past her and claimed it. He patted the space beside him for her to insert herself.

"When Charlene would return from her long rides, she would just plop down in that," Anton explained to Sara, who found a seat on the small sofa next to the little woman.

"I made up your room for you, clean sheets and all," Shelly said to Darrin and Sara.

"Aw, thanks!" Darrin liked the condo. His mom's art hung on all the walls along with many photos from her adventures. A portrait of Darrin was hanging over the dining table. It was a painting Charlene did from her favourite photo of Darrin. He was standing in front of an earth toned temple in Marrakesh. Sara had seen the photo before, but the painting brought new life to it. 'She was so talented" Sara was impressed.

There was so much for Sara to take in. Shelly gave her a quick tour. The view from the 11th floor was beautiful. You could see the city in its best light. The sun greeted the apartment at early morning and stayed until almost noon. The natural light illuminated Charlene's paintings with colour and life. They mostly portrayed Black women. She had a few self-portraits in the hall. The colours were vibrant and alluring. Sara was amazed at the beauty of each painting. The bookshelf had many books and magazines. There was even a shelf of old records. Anton claimed he was the lover of vinyl. Charlene and Anton were a cross of old people and retro hipsters.

"She was your dance teacher?" Sara asked, remembering the things Darrin had told her.

Shelly smiled. "Yes, when I was only ten years old. We loved Miss Charlene, she would let us stay over and play with all her wigs and costumes. She was beautiful, and when she danced, everyone was amazed. Her dance studio, which was where she lived, was like a big playhouse. Then I came to visit her in Montreal and gave her a ride back to Nova Scotia. The whole twelve hour drive she talked about how great Montreal was. So she offered me a room to get things together and I stayed with them for Like…six or seven months. Those were the best times. Charlene was funny and Anton used to laugh at everything we did. We were always laughing." Shelly continued to smile, thinking about her friend. "I never left Montreal after that. I got married and Vern, my husband, we come over often to be with Charlene and Anton. See that painting? That's us," she pointed to the lovely oil painting of two women eating ice cream on the beach. "We went to Italy together for Charlene's 55th birthday, just the two of us." Shelly was so proud. She knew that anyone lucky enough to spend time with Charlene was truly fortunate to breath in her wisdom and love.

In the afternoon, Anton and Darrin went to talk to someone about renting a hall for the memorial. Sara and Shelly stayed in the living room, going through some of Charlene's photo books and digital prints.

"I cannot believe how many photos she has," Sara marvelled.

"Charlene was crazy about photos, even before the digital age. She said even as a young girl she always documented stuff. She has photos of my old dance classes somewhere among these," Shelly informed everyone.

Shelly held up a picture of Charlene holding a one-month-old Darrin. "Look at this little peanut," Shelly teased. Sara reached for the picture and looked at the earliest photo of the man she loved.

"You can take what you want, make a pile for Darrin," Shelly insisted

Sara nodded, placing that picture beside her. Charlene had documented every part of her life. Pictures of her with many dance students, friends, her family, her travels and bike rides. It was truly overwhelming looking into her life as a stranger. She tried to remember all the things Darrin had said about his mom. She thought they were the ramblings of a child who loved his mother but now she could see that everyone loved this woman.

Toronto

Marlon Styles was set to perform at the Blue Light Lounge, an old bar in the heart of Toronto's newest gentrified neighbourhood. The owner of the bar, Terry Roach, was super excited. He remembered seeing Marlon perform at many Toronto events over the years. He had heard that Marlon's voice still had the same soft, sweet sound as always. Terry's father had often bragged about a having Marlon sing at his wedding before Terry was born. The idea of having Toronto's most legendary voice perform at his club brought him great joy.

Terry invited all his friends to his bar that evening. He had waited a long time to shake the hand of this entertainer, and tonight it was finally happening. He had his people put a flyer together with a photo Marlon's agent had sent. He was still a fine-looking man. Terry asked Andrea, his dependable bar manager, to post the flyers all over the building.

The photo was a few years old. Marlon had lost ten pounds since it had been taken. His life had been through many changes and the wear of it was showing through the musician's face and body. But in the promo picture, he was still a sexy, youthful singer with diamond studs in both ears, a contrast to his rich, dark colour and shaped-up hair fade.

"I know this man had all the girls tossing panties," Andrea teased, she did the usual stuff to prepare for the night's entertainment. She fixed up the backstage room with refreshments and stocked the mini fridge. Marlon Styles was a bit before her time, but Andrea's mother and two aunts were coming. Her mother claimed Marlon went to middle school with her cousin Rolland. Her aunties both said they had a huge crush on the singer back in the day.

Terry had a promotional company blast the event on many social media sites. He expected a full house. Even at 66, Marlon Styles was a presence. He was tall and thin. He had a shiny bald head with an owl's grey beard, all trimmed and shaped. His clothes had definitely been with him for a bit. His shiny shirt hung on him like he was a human hanger.

Andrea greeted him at the door and brought him his choice of drink before she prepared the stage for his sound check. Like the pro he was, he shook hands with his hired musicians. They were all young and he didn't know any of them, but after a bit of conversation, he learned his bassist was actually the grandson of a musician Marlon knew years ago. Marlon was used to feeling old, as though nothing is what it was. He saw so few people from his best days in the club scene. His generation of fans were mostly gone, or they didn't make it out anymore. He missed the good old days, but knew they were gone forever. Retiring as a singer was a constantly occurring thought, but he knew without a gig, he was as good as dead.

The young musicians all scattered after the sound check, leaving Marlon alone with only the club staff. Andrea continued to clear the bar and cut up the fruit and garnishes.

"Are you sticking around?" Andrea shouted across the room.

Marlon looked in the bar's direction.

"Got nowhere to be. Scared if I leave …." his voice trailed

Andrea went to the kitchen and had the cook put a nice dish together for the old-time entertainer.

He sat quietly at the bar, eating a chicken dish with roasted vegetables and a slice of pecan pie while he waited for showtime.

"This is nice of you," Marlon smiled at Andrea in a way he hoped showed gratitude.

"No worries, you still have a couple hours before the show. You can hang out here at the bar with me," she smiled.

Marlon spent almost his whole life in bars and night clubs making chat with bartenders and waitresses, eating special off the menu meals, talking shop with players and musicians.

"Can I take a pic for my Instagram?" she asked sweetly.

Marlon gave a chuckle. "I don't think any of your friends will even know who I am."

He leaned forward and pointed his best side at her phone. Andrea flashed her whole spectrum of teeth and Marlon gave what was to be his last smile of the night.

"You're a legend in these parts," she grinned.

Andrea was beautiful. She had natural thick hair pulled into a puff bun. She wore glasses that might be more for fashion than function. Marlon revelled in the flattery as he moved his empty dinner plate aside and pulled the pie towards him. It was only after he finished his pie that Andrea shoved her phone into his hand to show him the comments and likes their photo had gained in popularity online. Some women had been quite generous with their admiration of the singer.

Marlon took his phone out and tried to log in. He wanted to add this beautiful pic to his page so his fans could see. Before he had a chance to do that, the flashing notifications stole his attention. Andrea saw a rapid change in his demeanour.

"Marlon, what is it, Mister Styles?"

Andrea felt horrible as she watched this old man cry openly at the bar. She couldn't image what could possibly have happened in the span of the last three minutes.

"Come backstage, I have your bar set up and you can rest. Come on Mr. Styles, I will stay with you," she coaxed.

Helping him off his stool in the empty bar, Andrea guided him backstage to a small room next to the stage area. She reached into the mini fridge and pulled out a beer. Marlon didn't take the drink. He sunk into the sofa, looking at his phone again, and sobbed out loud. With no shame or guilt, this elderly man wept. Not knowing what to do, Andrea left the room. *He needs a few moments of privacy*, she thought to herself, standing outside the room.

Montreal

Vern Shales entered the Griffintown high-rise without buzzing up the apartment. He knew Abdul well and had many deep philosophical conversations with him in the lobby over the years.

"Just bringing some things for my wife," said Vern, holding up an overnight bag. Abdul nodded. Vern married Shelly six and a half years ago. He and his wife had been steady visitors to the condo.

"It's a terrible shame. I have known Anton and Charlene for a few years now. I was here at the desk when they first came to see the condo. We were a brand-new building at the time. She loved it." Abdul made conversation while Vern waited for the elevator.

Abdul looked like he'd lost his best friend. Both men were quiet, thinking about Charlene. Vern gave a small nod and headed into the lift. As he approached the apartment door, he heard the hearty laugh of his wife inside. He tapped on the door and waited. Shelly opened the door, throwing herself into her husband's arms.

"Sounds like a party in here," Vern said, entering the living room.

"Not quite." Darrin greeted Vern and introduced Sara.

Vern was a tall slender man. Sara was surprised that Shelly and her husband were such a contrast to each other in so many ways.

"I brought you some things I thought you might need," Vern held up the small overnight bag.

Shelly grabbed her bag. Vern had brought some of her essentials.

"Thanks so much, I was wearing Charlene's panties!" she teased. Everyone chuckled except Sara, who couldn't quite figure out if the small woman was joking or serious.

Darrin brought out a bottle he had stashed with his things in his mother's storage. He had many bottles stored in her place for celebrations upon his return. He decided to bring them all up to the apartment and celebrate his mother with high priced spirits.

"Stay for a drink," he convinced Vern. Darrin was always the friendly barman. Few people could resist Darrin's hospitable nature. He had a way with people, a kind of international charm.

"Yes, please, we are going to be up all night choosing photos for Char's memorial and we all know Char had over a billion great pics to choose from," Shelly added.

"My lady was not camera shy!" Anton joked.

"That's for sure! I spent my whole childhood facing the lens," Darrin laughed, remembering the many times he had faced her camera or phone and was asked to smile.

Shelly had put together some nibbles to help soak up the very strong bottle of whiskey Darrin had put out. The mood was light as everyone spoke of Charlene and what her legacy would look like. Anton was surprised when he heard Abdul ringing up.

"We have another guest? Maybe it is a party!" Vern joked.

"Are things always so lively at these times?" Sara asked.

"She's not used to Black folk yet," Darrin teased, bringing on a flash of blush across his girlfriend's face. Minutes later there was a soft tap on the door. Shelly skipped past everyone to get it.

Pierre LaVie stood in the door frame. Anton immediately went to him and hugged him like they were brothers. Pierre knew that if anyone understood the depth of his pain, it would be Anton. They had known her most intimately and for the longest time of any others. Pierre was attempting to hold his pain on the inside, trying not to make eye contact with Anton. Pierre was a handsome man. He had a well-kept salt and pepper beard. His eyes were soulful and telling. Charlene used to tell Shelly, "I like good looking men and all my men are fine." No one could dispute that fact.

"Pierre, come on in," Shelly lead Pierre into the living room. She made introductions to Darrin and Sara. Vern nodded a hello. Darrin and Pierre had never met, but often heard stories about each other from Charlene. The two men stood face to face for a moment.

"I am glad you came by," Shelly leaned over and said to Pierre. This eased the broken-hearted man. She could see he was in great pain. Shelly remembered when Charlene first started seeing Pierre. It was about ten years ago. She was smitten like a schoolgirl. Pierre was six years younger than Charlene. He was a gorgeous athlete trainer from Cameroon. His French accent was quite beautiful. Charlene's relationship with Pierre was very different from hers and Anton's. "He is my French lover. We eat croissants, drink wine and listen to music. He is like a vacation," she once said.

"Your whole life is a vacation," Shelly had replied.

Pierre was comfortable in the apartment. He had been there so often over the years. He accepted a glass of the golden liquor Charlene's son had offered him and sat quietly listening to her closest people share their thoughts and memories.

Toronto

Andrea couldn't believe her eyes as she watched the legendary artist fall to pieces in front of her. She did her best to keep him calm. Marlon unfortunately could not keep it together. His whole body oozed his grief and sorrow. He made no attempt to pull himself together.

"Mr Styles," Andrea sat down beside him.

Marlon's sobs continued. He covered his face with the shiny sleeve of his oversized shirt. His pain was real, and it was raw. Every second a new memory would bring him into a new realm of pain and despair.

Terry entered the green room. "The band has arrived" he spoke softly. A conversation in body language passed between Terry and his bar manager.

Andrea nodded and said they just need a few more minutes.

"Mr. Styles, I know you are in so much pain right now, and if you don't want to do this event tonight, I understand." Her voice was gentle and soothing.

"She... she was the love of my life," the words were tiny when they left his quivering lips.

Andrea held the old man's hand. She could only imagine what this news has meant to him.

"I am so sorry. You were in love with this lady?" she asked, helping him into a chair.

Marlon stopped crying and almost laughed. "I loved her since I was 20 years old, can you imagine? I am 66 and I never stopped loving her." He put away his phone, which he had held tightly for the last half hour. "Look," he insisted.

Andrea looked at the Instagram page he had open on the phone, showing a lovely fair skinned woman. She was young in the picture. It was maybe 20 years before. She had a beautiful smile as she stared into the camera.

"She was beautiful." Andrea smiled warmly.

"She was indeed. She was everything," he sobbed. Marlon pulled a white cloth from his pocket to wipe each tear and its wet path from his face.

"Mr. Styles, the band is here, and soon the doors will open, do you think you can go on tonight? Are you able to lock this heavy pain away for just a couple hours? If you do that, I promise I am going to help you with everything you need to do to get through this." Andrea's words sounded like the lifeline he needed. She felt so bad for the broken man before her. Marlon had met and dealt with many club owners and managers over the years, but this young lady was different from all of them. She was an angel. He wanted to pull himself together, if only just to impress this woman. Many had idolized her.

Marlon slowly nodded. "You're are a sweet girl. I can, and I will. Cause young lady, Marlon Styles is a professional." He started moving his old bones and attempted to stand up. Andrea assisted him.

"I am truly sorry, for your loss," she reiterated.

"Bring the band in, as they say...the show must go....on." Marlon wiped his face once again. His bony hands pressed his suit jacket as he put it on. He spoke to the musicians when they entered the backstage room.

That night was without a doubt one of the greatest performances of Marlon Styles' career. He sang originals, he did the classics, he danced and charmed the audience. His last song was gentle and romantic, and Marlon made every person at the Blue Light lounge feel more than they thought they could. Terry was happy with the night and promised himself to give Marlon a steady gig in the future. After his last note was hit, Marlon left the stage while the band finished up the set without him. Andrea couldn't find the singer anywhere after the show. He and the flimsy coat he came in with were gone. Terry found Andrea backstage after everyone had left.

"He's gone?" Terry appeared perplexed. "He didn't even wait for his pay," he added.

Andrea took the little yellow pay envelope and signed for it.

"I will take it to him tomorrow" She promised. Terry knew and trusted Andrea. She was a very responsible lady. He knew of her virtues from the many times he had tried to seduce her. Andrea would have nothing to do with him. He respected the strength of her will and she was great with the staff. Andrea took her job very seriously, so much that she was often accused of not living a life outside of work. It was true. Since her divorce, she had done nothing but throw herself into her job. She promised herself once this big show was past, she would do something fun. Maybe take a little winter vacation.

Chapter 4

Making plans

Helen was so happy. Her son was coming home for the week. She remembered how excited she was to become an empty nest parent. She had such plans for projects and continued learning, but once the boys left, everything went quiet. She had her father downstairs, but he was still busy in his own way. Ash was an independent senior. He had his own friends and activities. He didn't need Helen for much. He wasn't a fan of her newfound healthy living. He was never going to leave his strong, Southern meat-eating ways behind. He rarely came upstairs. He bought his own groceries, cooked his own food and cleaned his own space.

At 7:30 in the evening, her oldest son, Kevin, entered the house with a huge duffle bag. He had even started growing a beard, she noticed. Helen was so excited to see her first born. She was a proud mama with two college boys. Kevin was the athlete of the family. He played football and did well in Track in his younger, slimmer days. It had only been four short months since she last had seen her boy and he was easily a good 15 pounds up from then.

"Look at you! You got facial hair and you don't seem to be starving, "she teased.

Kevin was thick like his grandfather. Not fat, just large. Secretly, Helen couldn't wait to introduce her son to some of the vegan meals she had been learning to make.

Kevin released his mom from a hearty bear hug. "I been eating alright," he grinned.

"That your laundry?" her tone changed.

"Naw, not all of it," he confessed with a slight smirk.

"Go put it in the laundry room, I will have it done by tomorrow. Then go downstairs and see your granddad. He hasn't been doing so well lately." She kissed her boy once more on his rough beard.

That was not news he wanted to hear. Kevin loved being around his granddad. When he was small, Ash used to take the boys to the racetrack to meet his granddad's race car friends. They never got to see Ash race, he had retired before they were born. Kevin did his special knock on his granddad's door. The same combination of raps on the door he did as a kid.

"That you, Kevvy?" He heard the old guy rattling around the room and then slowly opening the door. Ash grabbed his grandson into a big hug. They were nearly the same size now.

"Look at you, get in here!" Ash's mood had done a 180 degree turn just seeing his favourite grandson. "So glad you're back. For how long? A week?" Ash asked with intensity.

"Yep, should be enough time for us to catch a few movies. Maybe see a car show," Kevin suggested.

"Yeah. That sounds nice," Ash pushed a smile.

It didn't take Kevin any time to see his granddad was not his usual self. He seemed distracted.

"What's wrong, granddad?" Kevin pressed, knowing his grandfather's normal temperament to be relaxed and content. Ash never bothered anyone and always had a smile when his family was around.

"So, I need to ask you something, and it's got to stay between you and me... Not like the kind of secret you can't tell your mom because someone is hurting you. It's more like my own privacy thing. Can you do that?" Ash pleaded.

Kevin didn't hesitate. He was honoured his granddad trusted him like that. He knew whatever was going to be asked of him would help make things better. Kevin looked at his granddad, trying to ascertain what could possibly be bothering the old man.

"Sure, granddad," Kevin was eager to help. "Anything." he said warmly.

Ah breath a relief sigh. He knew his grandson would answer as such.

"You got a passport? "he asked.

Memphis

Marcy brought back James's laundry and a container leaking out the aroma of food from his favourite rib joint. She even included a slice of red velvet cake that he should not be eating.

James was truly grateful as he thanked her. He poured himself a big glass of Mountain Dew and parked his aging bones in his favourite lounge chair in front of the television with the food.

"So, you're good?" she asked after putting his clothes down. She grabbed her jacket and headed for the door.

"Um-hmm," he responded, as he continued to savour his mashed potatoes. Henry's Ribs made the best mash potatoes. Marcy sure knew his love for good food.

Less than a minute after hearing the porch door close, a scream from Marcy brought him to his feet. James rushed to the back door to find Marcy on the ground at the bottom of his front steps. His busty neighbour, Mrs. Thompson from across the street, already had her front door open and watched on.

Marcy was in tears. Her foot rested on the first step as she cried out.

"I missed the last step," she cried. He helped get her up and back into the house. Marcy wasn't a large woman, but she could afford to lose a few pounds.

"I have been down those stairs so many times in my life, I can't believe this!" She wailed on.

James propped her up on the sofa and put a blanket on the stool where she rested her leg.

"I am going to get some ice for it.," He moved quickly towards the kitchen. With care and concern, he wrapped her leg in a kitchen towel and an ice pack. Then he brought her a tall glass of sweet tea.

"Are you okay?" he asked attentively.

Marcy smiled. She was enjoying the attention. James often acted indifferent towards her. But now, on this day, she was seeing the old James; the man she married and wanted a life with. That was a dream that had already failed and left her with a deep hole in her heart.

"Been a very long time since you were so nice to me," she teased.

James felt the sting of her words. He knew he had not done Marcy kindly over the years. She had been a good woman and taken great care of him during their short marriage and after.

"Marcy, you know I had lots of love for you, we just..." he didn't know what else to say.

"Fell out of love," she finished his thought.

"Well, we really didn't have much in common from the start, but I always loved the way you took care of me, Marcy. I really should have let you know that. You're a fine woman." James felt relieved to tell her his thoughts on that day. The same day he learned about Charlene Reese's death.

It all felt a bit too much. Marcy was unsure of what to do with his praise. She attempted to change the subject and steer attention away from herself.

"What about this friend of yours, a lady friend?" Marcy asked with genuine concern.

James was quiet for a long time. He finally took a deep breath began to explain the story he held inside his soul. Marcy forgot she had asked by the time she heard his voice.

"Her name is Charlene Reese," he said with a long exhale.

Marcy sat patiently waiting for James to spill the beans on the mystery woman.

"You remember, I told you I was living in Texas, after my second marriage to Linda, long time ago? Anyhow, it was early in the online movement, before the Facebook or Instagram thing. We were all on this site, The planet of Black folk. I joined up, I guess out of boredom. Used to log on after work. It relaxed me. Have a drink and just..." James shrugged his shoulders.

"A dating site?" she asked.

'No, not at all, it was a group of unlikely people just talking about all subjects. Music, sex, politics, you name it. Anyhow, Charlene was in the group. Her code name was Lady Dance. She was a dancer. Fine looking woman. Red boned and foreign. I think a lot of guys in the group liked her. I did, she had a different outlook than the other girls."

"So, you all got together?" Marcy asked

"the group decided. Someone thought we should all meet up, have a gathering for the group in a city of choice. It was New York. She crossed the Canadian border and showed up. I remember being really excited to meet her.

Marcy removed the melted ice from her leg and gave James her attention.

"She was great, pretty much how I imagined. Fair skinned woman from Canada. She was attractive. I aint gonna lie to you, we spent some time alone together. I thought, it was what it was... she lived in another Country and I wasn't trying to get caught up again. It was literally just after my divorce. She went back to her home, life when on." he explained.

'That can't be all" Marcy pushed.

James chuckled. "Saw her a few more times, each time she seemed to be more and more free and in control. She came to one of our meets in, Georgia, not the one in New Orleans, and she told the group about her life and her lovers. They all got such a kick out of her stories and her sexual freedom," he smiled at the thought.

"I am sure you did too," Marcy challenged.

"I was scared." James stared off out the window

"Scared?" Marcy sounded sceptical.

"I didn't know how to play that game; I just withdrew a bit. Marcy, I know a bit about life. I have cheated and been cheated on. But her level of life and honesty, I just really didn't know how to file it in my head. It made sense, but in a way I was not altogether sure about." He tried to connect his feelings to the words.

Marcy nodded, knowing there was more to the story but willing to wait for it. She was surprised. She thought James was so worldly and adventurous in his life.

"You were not in love with her?" she pressed.

"I loved her; she was an incredible woman. But no, I was...infatuated by the idea of her. We remained close over the years, but not intimately. I mean, not sexually. t's been about eight years since I have seen her, or any of the group really. We don't talk as much as we used to. But Reesy sent me a trinket in the post a few years back. It was a hand painted shot glass. She was very artistic. I assumed she made one for the whole group. She was a thoughtful woman." he paused, looking wistful.

Marcy took the ice pack from her ankle again. Her whole foot was numb from the cold.

"So, this trip you're talking about, it's for her funeral?" she asked.

James nodded.

"I gotta go to pay respects. And I really want to meet this Anton dude, her life partner I've been hearing about for all these years. He seems too good to be real."

"I can come, if you like," Marcy offered

"You are going to stay right here and rest up that ankle," James insisted. Marcy wanted to protest. She had never felt so close to James, he had never shared so much of himself before. This was the time she wanted to be there for him and with him. He was traveling with such feelings and she was stuck home with a foot unable to support her weigh even if he allowed her to accompany him on this journey. Marcy stayed quiet, allowing James to work through his thoughts and feelings. He was deeply affected by this, and she wondered what the outcome would look like for them once he returned.

Nassau

It was uncommonly cold on the Island. Shirley had wrapped herself in a warm knitted sweater as she put the kettle on to make herself a cup of tea. The thoughts of Charlene's death still filled her mind. She waited for her girlfriend Dory to come over. Dory worked for the book shop in the tourist area of the Island. The Tropical bookstore was her grandfather's shop. It would be another two hours before Dory would be off her shift. Shirley knew she had a lot to tell her friend about Charlene and Derrick. "I am going to need more than tea," she thought to herself. Grabbing her purse, Shirley left her apartment to acquire a bottle of the island's famous rum. Another hour later, when Dory arrived, the rum was already open and tasted. Shirley was in a pleasant mood.

"You started the party without me," Dory teased.

"Maybe a bit of liquid courage," Shirley replied. She couldn't believe the nervousness she felt.

Dory's eyes shot up. "This is going to be interesting!" She pulled out a chair at the kitchen island and poured herself a glass of the tropical poison. Dory had been there for Shirley for over a decade. The two met at the hair salon and found they had so much in common. Now they ran support for each other in stressful times.

"Girl, I know you got things on your mind," Dory settled in for a session.

Shirley gave a deep sigh before starting the conversation. She knew Dory Layne couldn't imagine the spinning thoughts that occupied her headspace.

"Well I never talked to you about any of this, because it wasn't really my thing to tell you, it was Derrick's, and it was so different from what we usually talk about or even how we live. Since he died, you know what they say about things coming to life when there is a death," Shirley let out another big sigh.

Dory looked seriously at her friend. "What is it?" She was not sure the level of concern needed.

Shirley laughed, "You know that I was with Derrick for ten years, right?" Shirley started. "I wasn't his first wife, or first love or first anything."

Dory nodded. "I was there when you met him, Shirley. He would have been my husband if I had worn my red pumps that night!" Dory teased.

They never got tired of that joke.

"Right, well when I met him, as you know, he had been traveling around the world, working offshore here and there. He worked and travelled and then retired here on the Island. We fell in love, and well, you know he was here with me until he died." Shirley summed up her life with Derrick.

"Yeah, I know all this. Wait! Shirley...please don't tell me this man has children still surfacing, did someone call you?" Dory's voice shot up in pitch. She shook her head from side to side letting her braids hit her in the face.

Shirley laughed. "No, nothing like that."

Dory sipped her drink, waiting on Shirley.

"He had this friend, from his earlier days. Her name was Charlene Reese." Shirley started.

Dorey nodded "Ok,"

"She was very special to him," Shirley continued.

"Special? He was in love with her, that what you mean?" Dory was trying her best to stay patient and listen. Her instinct told her to keep pushing for Shirley to spill the beans.

"Not exactly, he like, just, I don't know, he worshipped her. He thought the sun rose and set in her eyes," Shirley continued.

Dory knew Shirley was struggling with what she wanted to say. Dory stared at Shirley for a few seconds, not sure if she should laugh or not, before saying, "Okay, okay, sorry, so he knew this woman, and he worshipped her ass, okay? So, what, was he stalking her, was he cheating on you?" Dory sat up ready to be supportive, or a gangster if needed.

Shirley shook her head. She wasn't sure where the conversation was going, or even where she wanted it to go.

"I don't think you get what I am saying," Shirley struggled.

Dory put down her glass and gave Shirley all her attention. "You are not saying anything Shirley, that is the problem"

Shirley inhaled and pushed a long breath out. "Charlene Reese... she was a badass bitch. Derrick was crazy about her and to be honest, so was I, and now she's gone. She died and I can't seem to stop thinking about it all." Shirley blurted out.

"Wow! Wasn't expecting that!" Dory refilled her glass.

"So, like what, a threesome?" Dory spoke before her brain had a chance to formulate her ideas.

"No!" Shirley said too loudly. Then gave another big sigh.

"You knew Derrick, he was different from most brothers around here. He thought differently, talked differently. He had ideas and beliefs that I had never thought of before I met him. He had been married three times. He lived 50 years before I met him. He travelled and knew a lot about life. When we met, he said, "Shirley, I can't marry another woman and continue on like I always have." I hoped he meant he was not going to be a cheating S.O.B., but he had bigger plans of what he wanted from this marriage," she continued.

"What, was it something kinky? Did he want weekly threesomes? He looked like the type," Dory whispered loudly. Shirley fell out laughing. She knew Dory was capable of a degree of crazy and she was only getting started.

"No, silly, he didn't want nothing kinky, nothing like that. He wanted a relationship where he was free to say what he wanted to say, be transparent and not lie about what he or I was feeling. At first, I said yes, you know, just to appease him. But he wanted to be able to talk about the women in his past without judgment or jealousy, and to be honest, it wasn't easy. He would tell me about his ex-wives, some of his affairs from back in the day, he would tell me about detailed things that I never thought a married couple should or would ever talk about. The more we talked, the more I relaxed. I trusted him with things I never thought I would tell a man. You know, my mama even told me not to tell a man about my past, said they would hold it against me, and throw it back at me, but it was freeing to speak to him about some of my pain and my desires." Shirley had been imitating her husband for years and felt closer to him when she did.

"He wanted to tell you about what, his conquests?" Dory's face turned sour.

"No, Dor, he wanted to share about people and places he had experienced and if I shut that part of him out, I knew we would drift apart. So, I opened up and listened, and to be honest, it made us so much closer. I knew so much about him and it helped me to talk more about myself. I never did that with any other man before, share my pain or even what I liked, because I thought you were never supposed to do that. So, he often would talk about this Charlene woman. He would bring her up from time to time, or he would see something on the computer and say, 'wow, Charlene just rode her bike across Canada,' or 'Charlene has an art exhibit in New York.' I would get jealous of how much he talked about her or thought about her, but that was the gift I had committed to giving him. And then one day he says, 'Shirley, I got some great news, Charlene Reese is coming to Nassau.' She was coming to the Island on a vacation and he was taking us all out for a meal."

"She came, here for a vacation?" Dory refilled her glass.

Shirley nodded, still not sure how much further she was going to go with the conversation.

"What was she like?" Dory asked, adding more ice to her drink.

Shirley continued, "She was everything he had said she was. Meeting her made me understand him better, if you can imagine that. We were going to meet at the Bahamian place, Derrick loved that spot. He was like a tourist sometimes. Give him a drink in a pineapple and he was happy. I was nervous and changed about five times, so we were running a bit late. Charlene and her man were already cozy in a booth when we arrived. She looked like she was no stranger to vacations. She wore this bright pink and yellow halter dress, I couldn't imagine being over forty and wearing something like that, but she looked beautiful with her wild, curly, frizzy afro. The man was gorgeous, like movie-star-good-looking. They were just seated there like a photo from Ebony magazine."

Dory smiled, knowing the rum was hitting Shirley nicely.

"He was French, like real French! He greeted you with that double kiss and his accent, whew girl! His name was Pierre, the whole scene was right out of a movie." Shirley's memory of that night was vividly clear.

Pierre leaned in and kissed Shirley on both sides of her face. She seemed a bit embarrassed by this gesture. Usually the rich French men who travelled to the island on business greeted people this way, but never had she had a handsome man like Pierre touch her skin and say 'enchante' with such a sexy accent. She then caught a huge embrace from Charlene before she and Derrick took a seat.

Pierre was wearing a lose vacation shirt and walking shorts. Shirley tried not to look his way too often, but he was so striking. Charlene had on a beautiful pink and yellow sarong tied up like a halter dress, and was looking like a light-skinned Island girl herself.

Drinks arrived and their food order had been placed. Shirley sat next to Derrick, making small talk and advising on the best places to see around the Island. Shirley had too quickly finished her first tall drink of island punch when she started to loosen up some.

"So, you two are married?" *She asked, finally finding her voice.*

"No, my husband is back in Montreal," *Charlene said as the food arrived.*

Shirley could feel all the blood rush to her face. Pierre was trading the dishes the waiter had mixed up, as Derrick was adding an abnormal amount of hot sauce to his plate.

"Wait, 'scuse me?" *Shirley finally spoke. She felt like she was waiting on a punchline.*

Charlene placed her fork down and wiped her mouth before speaking.

"It's too bad too, because he would love this Island," *Charlene continued.*

Shirley looked at Derrick, who just smiled, then over to Pierre, who nodded in agreement.

"Wait, ..scuse me?" *Shirley was now at a total loss for her words.*

Charlene looked over at Derrick.

"You never told her?" *she asked.*

Derrick laughed.

"I thought it would be more fun this way!" *Charlene let out a laugh and Pierre smirked.*

Chewing her first bite of fish, Charlene cleared her throat with a big swig of wine.

"Okay, so my husband is back home in Montreal. He is not very into travel, so I came with Pierre, who does enjoy traveling and new places." *Charlene said.*

Pierre nodded again, as if agreeing with the pleasant weather.

"So, Pierre, is your..." *Shirley appeared flustered and confused.*

"...Lover." *Charlene said the matter-of-factly.*

Now it was Shirley who needed a drink, and praise the Lord, the waiter put another tall glass of island punch in front of her. 'Just in time,' Shirley thought.

"Shirley, I am in a polyamorous relationship, which means I love and have relationships with more than one person. I am not monogamous. Pierre and I have been in a relationship for five years now. My husband, the man I reside with in Montreal, and I both consentingly have lovers outside of our relationship."

"So...your husband, at home, knows you are both here together?" *Shirley clarified.*

Pierre was the one to answer. "He drove us to the airport."

By this time, Shirley was in quite a state. She looked to Derrick for help, but somehow, he was enjoying the info session.

It was at that moment she wondered if Derrick and this woman were having Polyamorous relations; if that was the reason they were all having this meal. A panic started to rise, and Shirley could feel sweat running down her face. She abruptly excused herself and rushed towards the bathroom. A few minutes later Charlene joined her. Shirley rushed into the stall hoping Charlene would not see her crying.

"Shirley, I am sorry if I...if we somehow offended you. I can only image what you must be thinking. But we aren't here to intrude on your life or impose. I just wanted to see an old friend, the island he talks of and the wonderful woman he loves."

Shirley exited the stall. She wiped her face and took out her lipstick.

"That is really why you are here?" *she asked.*

Charlene nodded.

"So, you and Derrick?"

Charlene shook her head. "...a long time ago, and it didn't work out. He went on with his life, and I went on with mine."

"So, you are not lovers?" *Shirley asked.*

"No, he is a friend. A dear friend who I enjoy catching up with and talking to." *Charlene declared*

"I guess I am being silly," *Shirley admitted.*

"Not at all, I can't believe he didn't even tell you. Derrick knows about my lifestyle and how I live."

"That's him, though," *Shirley laughed, as the two women exited the bathroom and returned to the table. They found Derrick very amused by it all. Shirley loosened up after her third refill of island punch.*

Shirley refreshed Nora's drink. They laughed at the simplicity of it. "... And that was the first time I laid eyes on Charlene Reese."

"She was sweet and genuine. We spent one more day with them on the beach. They were as normal as any couple, when you don't think of the man she had at home. Afterwards, we exchanged Facebook info and I could see her whole life. I saw her husband, who was every bit as gorgeous as the Frenchman. I followed her journey and her accomplishments. Eventually I began to see what Derrick saw. She's just this easy-going, free-spirited woman."

"Why are you telling me all this now, is she coming here? "Dory asked.

Shirley shook her head.

"Someone just called to say she died," Shirley answered.

Boston

Twenty-four hours after hearing about the death of Charlene Reese, Michael Sylvia was taken to the hospital in an ambulance. A neighbour had called the paramedics after seeing the seventy-eight-year-old collapsed on his front doorstep. Michael was distraught and confused when he received the news about Charlene. They had been friends for so long. He had reached out to Charlene at least once a week for almost four decades. With a suitcase in hand, he rushed out of his house on Convent Avenue. He had assumed the blinding pain he felt when he hit the cool air was grief. Before he knew what was happening, he felt his body give way and he fell.

Michael had been sick for some time, and his body couldn't take him on the journey his heart had desired. He arrived at St. Paul's Hospital early Thursday morning. He was admitted by the afternoon. The doctor gave orders to make the old gentleman as comfortable as possible. The staff kept a close watch on the elderly man whose life was nearing the end. Michael was scared and worried. He laid in the cold hospital sheets with his sorrows and pain. The flickering florescent light put him to sleep. He dreamed about better days. He dreamed about his "caramel muse".

Charlene was excited to be invited to Vegas and to be Michael's companion. As soon as he was accepted to the conference, he e-mailed Charlene and invited her. He knew how these functions were. You finished the workshops and then you ate alone and watched something sad on the television in the hotel room. He knew Charlene would make the trip that much more exciting. She had flown in to meet him at the Flamingo hotel. She sat propped up at the bar with her small carry-on, waiting for him.

Michael was quite the dapper man. He was distinguished and well-groomed, many would say.

"My lady," he greeted her formally.

Charlene broke into a huge smile and jumped up off her stool.

Michael was a wee bit embarrassed when Charlene grabbed him and hugged him. But that feeling was lost as he pulled away and looked at the stunning woman before him. Charlene was 49 years old and still looked 30. She had a smooth, perfect, tanned complexion, her skin still soft and youthful. She had never "let herself go". That was what he adored about this woman, she just kept getting better.

He was guiding her up to his room when he asked, "You only brought that little suitcase; how will you be able to take home all the gifts I have for you?"

Michael had emptied the contents of his suitcase on one of the beds. He had brought her dresses, shirts, sexy leggings, even shoes!

It was like Christmas for Charlene. She was like a child going through the beautiful presents, trying things on and modelling. Charlene had been receiving lovely gifts for years from Michael. He was in the fashion industry and really cared about seeing the right things on the right people. Charlene was always the right people.

Their relationship was just that. He loved to dress her. She loved taking pictures. Charlene and Michael had a great three days in Vegas. She walked around the glittery town taking photographs and selfies while he attended his business conference. They dined at night and even took in a show.

Michael was grateful that his muse was so free in her life that she could do these things with him.

Chapter 5

Toronto

Andrea was sure the address she had written on an envelope was incorrect. The building was run-down. She followed the raggedy looking carpet to the end of the hall and knocked on the door numbered 519. This area of town was inhabited mostly by new immigrants and low-income residents, but a few buildings were designated as apartments for the elderly.

Noise from the apartment across the hall got louder, so Andrea knocked again. A short time after, she saw Marlon poke his head through a half-opened door. He smiled at the sight of his new friend.

Marlon opened the door to allow Andrea's entrance. The apartment was not as poor-looking on the inside. Marlon had large paintings and photos of Black musicians and entertainers decorating the walls. There were a few instruments placed around the sitting room. The dark wooden furniture and area mat made the place feel warm. Marlon offered up his sitting chair, a big recliner with a grey throw covering the back. He took a seat on the well-worn sofa beside her. She could tell he really was happy to see her.

"Can I get you a drink? I have orange juice, orange pop, oh, and I have mint tea," he smiled warmly.

"That sounds great... a mint tea." Andrea was happy to sit and take in all the decorations of the cozy apartment. Marlon was boiling water in the kitchen while still maintaining the conversation.

'Sorry for leaving like that last night," he apologised.

"I totally understand, I was just so happy you were able to sing and get through it. Everyone was so impressed with your show," she added.

Marlon returned to the room with a tray bearing two cups of tea and a small plate with a few cookies on it.

Andrea placed his pay envelope on the table in front of him.

"Thank you, you are a sweet girl to come down here to bring me this," he smiled.

There were photos everywhere of Marlon on stage, Marlon with other celebrities, Marlon's awards.

"You've had quite a life" She said, while placing a framed picture back in the place it had lived. She sat back down in the seat beside him.

"It has been quite a ride," Marlon went into his mind's memories and smiled. He would have chosen no other existence. He had been singing since childhood.

"I performed all over the world, met so many people in the biz. I had quite a career. Hmm, looks like this is where it ends. A sad old man living in the low-income area of Toronto. But you know what, it was worse! This time last year, I didn't even have this much! I had nothing. But I am still here, as life has it, by the grace of God," he announced, louder than he had intended.

Andrea nodded. Her mother would have added an Amen, but Andrea was not as connected to the Religious mindset. She proclaimed herself to be spiritual and woke.

Marlon watched her face. She was a pretty young sister, perhaps 30 to 35 in years. He had an estranged son her age. His only son lived in London and had not spoken to him for years. This was the reality of many of his musician friends as well.

"You're not a Christian, are you?" he asked straight out. He was familiar with the defiance of God. She had the same look Charlene always had when he gave grace to his food or said a blessing. Charlene had no use for God, church or prayers. It was one of the biggest obstacles between them.

Andrea felt a small flush in her cheeks.

"No, I am not." She didn't want to offend him in his home. She remembered how sometimes older folks got mad when their heartfelt beliefs were denounced.

"Seems most people are not interested in believing anymore. I was a God-fearing man all my life. I always trusted in my God, but... she didn't, that was the first crack," he admitted.

"Charlene?" Andrea asked.

Marlon nodded. "I just received the memorial information," he said sadly. He showed Andrea the text Anton had sent him.

"It's in two days..." she read out loud, "...in Montreal," she added, as if that was a world away.

"Yes Montreal, where we fell in love. Well, I did anyhow. I was always in love with her."

He fell back into the memory, placing his large, dark hands over his face.

"Can you please do me a favour?" Marlon looked at Andrea with a helpless expression. Having to ask for help at his age was embarrassing. Marlon had only gotten back on his feet a few months ago. The gossip had him down and out with drug and alcohol abuse, but the truth was, he just fell into financial ruin and owed a lot of money. He had been homeless for a time, but still managed to keep his agent and get a few small gigs to pull himself back up with.

He placed his little laptop computer close to her and clicked on a site, then reached for his pay envelope.

"I can pay for the bus, but I don't have any credit cards anymore. If you book this for me, I can be spared a cold trip downtown to the bus station." He laid the money out for her next to the plate of cookies. The helpless expression covering this old man's face couldn't be denied.

"Sure, I am happy to help." She pulled the computer closer.

Andrea had booked Marlon on the 10 a.m. bus leaving the next morning and back two days later. He peeled off the ticket cost and placed it in her hands with absolute gratitude.

"You are a very kind woman. Thank you for taking care of this old man like you have." He touched her hand with great warmth and appreciation. Andrea smiled. "You're very welcome. Take care Mr. Styles," she hugged him and made her way out of his apartment building.

Charlotte, NC

Helen was happy her son was spending so much time down in the basement with his grandfather. It had scared her to see her father upset. He was not really the emotional type. He was pleasant and friendly, but didn't talk a lot about how he felt. He was just old school. She had come to understand that's how men from his era were. Helen was pleased Kevin was down there cheering her dad up. She could hear them laughing all night. They were so much alike. People always said Kevin took after his granddad. Kenny, her youngest, looked like her ex, but was sensitive and quiet, like her.

Placing Kevin's clean clothes on his bed like she had done for many years, Helen left for work after announcing her goodbyes throughout the house. Neither Ash nor her son responded.

"I will get them something special for supper," she thought as she got into the driver's seat of her Honda.

"Maybe I can grab something at Boston's after work." She laughed, knowing her father was not a fan of her vegan meals.

Montreal

Pierre took small sips of the smooth, honey-toned whiskey. He was not much of a drinking man, but had been known to enjoy a fine wine from time to time. He liked Charlene's son. She had talked a lot about Darrin and the bar he opened in the Netherlands, how they had travelled often together. He was easy-going like his mother. What Pierre wasn't prepared for was how much Darrin looked like Charlene. He had all the same facial expressions and even his laugh was identical to his mother's. It was almost too much to bear. Darrin was studying Pierre also. He had heard his mother mention him often. She really liked being with this French-speaking African man. He watched closely how Anton and Pierre interacted. They were like brothers.

Sara had taken a seat on the sofa beside Darrin. She had noticed a change in him. She was surprised at how comfortable and at ease he was here in his mother's home. Anton was in the big comfortable looking chair, which so clearly was his special seat in the house. He would get up and change the record when it ended, announcing the artist as he sat back down. Shelly was sprawled on the floor going through piles of photos. The albums and boxes piled high behind her.

"She sure did like to capture memories," Pierre smiled. "I thought I was a movie star when we went to Barbados, she documented every moment with her phone camera," he laughed, remembering his beloved on their island vacation.

Shelly sighed. "All these are so amazing. I can't decide on what's most appropriate to use at her memorial."

Darrin picked up the picture that attached itself to his sock. It was him sleeping on his mother's shoulders. They were on one of their many trips to Mexico.

"That's because they are all important. They are photos of her amazing life, they all matter," Darrin explained.

"When we first moved into the condo here, Charley was already in a relationship with Pierre. He helped us move here," Anton started.

Pierre nodded as the memory came back his mind also.

"So, I had gone out one night, probably to karaoke, and Charley came home with Pierre after I had left."

Now Pierre laughed ahead of the story. The memory was clear in his mind.

"And when they entered, Pierre had his arm around Charley. Poor Abdul, he saw them! So he kept an eye on the cameras. They had been kissing in the elevator and then at the door before she opened it. So Abdul made a copy of these 'indiscretions', I guess for me. But he liked Charley, of course, who didn't? So, he waited for her to come in alone one day, and he called her behind his desk to show her the footage. He was nervous and didn't want her to think he was blackmailing her. He said, 'I don't want any trouble, I just feel you should stop this fling you are having behind Mr. Henry's back. He is a decent man.'

"Charley loved all opportunities to flash her poly lifestyle card. She looked at him with that infamous Charley smile, the one where she looks like a devious five-year-old. Then she said, 'Abdul, can you make us a copy? I like the way I look in those videos!' Then she walked away. He never got over that!" Anton laughed harder, and as Pierre and Shelly joined in, Darrin grinned. He remembered his mom telling him that story when it happened. Sara wasn't the least bit amused. She was quite bothered, as if anyone had noticed.

"He figured it all out soon enough," Pierre laughed.

There was a short quietness before Shelly yelled out the answer to her own thoughts.

"We can use them all. Print up her digital pics and just cover the whole surface of the hall with them."

Darrin laughed. "That will be like, thousands and thousands of pictures!" He like the idea. He knew it was something his mother would be on board with.

"Let's do it!" he smiled

Anton smiled, "Then people can take the ones they want after," he suggested.

"Oui, c'est une bonne idee," "Pierre added. Montreal is a city where people speak both French and English at times. No one thought it was strange for Pierre to speak French. He felt more comfortable speaking his first language at that time.

Darrin joined Shelly on the floor as they started putting all the photos together.

Pierre looked to Anton, who seemed quiet and in his own world.

"She would be so happy right now, she loved being around people like this," Pierre said.

Anton nodded. "She was a happy woman."

Darrin nodded.

Sara had heard so many good things about Charlene. She found it hard to believe anyone was as amazing as everyone claimed this woman to be.

"You all make her out to be a saint. Didn't she ever get mad, or lash out? I am sure she had faults like everyone." Sara's accent made her words seem sharp and slightly offensive.

Darrin looked up, and Shelly shook her head.

"I have never had a fight with her, but Charlene was not a saint, she just... knew herself," Anton spoke.

"Her French was atrocious!" Pierre laughed, trying to bring back the nice mood.

"The thing about Charlene, she was good at many things. So, few people got to see her when she wasn't on top of her game. I met Charlene when I was only ten years old and she was the most amazing dancer to me. After that, she was like a mother and a sister and a best friend. She was funny and easy going, but she was also...alone. I don't know, you could only get so close to her, and we were very close." Shelly stopped to think about her words. "Am I even making sense?" she questioned.

"Yeah, she knew a lot of people, but she was also alone in her world," Anton added.

Darrin nodded. 'She was in a world where very few people understood her, her life, her vision. It was hard for her, but she pushed on."

Sara nodded, she had still so many reservations about this woman.

Darrin Continued, "I remember watching her paint. She was good when she started, but she would work daily to get better. She would throw half painted works away and get frustrated. But when she wanted to learn to do something, she did it. Same with her cycle training, she was out on her bike in any weather, just pushing herself."

"She was good at loving people," Pierre added.

"Yes," Shelly agreed.

"To Charlene!" Shelly held up her glass while Darrin rushed around to make sure everyone had a fresh top-off.

"I think I will go to bed," Sara said, before Darrin could pour her another drink. She got up and said good night to everyone. Pierre got up too, and followed Sara. When they reached the bedroom, Sara stopped.

"Excusez-moi, I know you are staying in the spare room. I just need to retrieve a few of my things," he appealed to her. Pierre stood in the door frame trying not to invade this fragile woman's space.

Sara stepped aside and pushed one of the larger suitcases against the wall. Pierre went straight into the closet. He reached down and found a man's toiletries bag. He opened the dresser drawer and pulled out some items, then he remembered something and went back to the closet and grabbed his house coat. He nodded a thank you and headed for the door.

"You stayed over here?" Sara asked. She knew Pierre was Charlene's lover, but didn't expect he actually spent time in their home.

He answered with a nod. "Every Thursday and sometimes Sunday." His answer was more like a memory recall then a statement.

He walked out of the room. The room that was filled with sacred memories of him and his lover. He realized he may never see it again. Sara closed the door firmly behind Pierre. She had more questions, but didn't want to be seen as nosy.

The rest of the group stayed up talking and reminiscing about the lovely Charlene well into the early morning hours. Pierre fell asleep on the sofa while Shelly and Darrin continued to go through Charlene's photos and memorabilia.

Boston

Michael Sylva wasn't Deborah's favourite patient. He was an old-timer dying. He didn't have any visitors. She did feel a small bit of pity for the man. He had been in the hospital for the past two days and complained about everything. He had a running temperature of 90. She had seen many elderlies before him run a high temperature and then systematically their main functions would shut down. Mr. Silva didn't appear to be concerned about his pending death or lack of visitors. He constantly babbled on about a woman, which Deborah found odd. Debora was a lesbian woman who had prided herself on her ever-fictional "gay-dar".

"He is an old fag, if ever there was one!" she joked with her co-worker.

Deborah was called to her boss's office soon as she started her shift. She assumed her old man had passed in the night and she would have to do the paperwork to start the shift.

Doctor Neeman introduced Deborah to Leesa Barnes.

"Leesa comes from Ohio, and has transferred here, to Boston. She will do rounds with you. So just give her a run down on how things are done here." He dismissed the two women with a quick nod as he returned to his desk.

Leesa was nice enough. Deborah was surprised she had been chosen to train her. She didn't think any of the head staff liked her much. She was what people called "a bit rough around the edges".

"Welcome to the D wing," Deborah passed her the day's files.

"We check in on all these patients before 10:30." She squeezed hand sanitizer into her palm.

"We start with Michael Sylva, a 78-year-old African American. He has high temperature and the early stages of liver failure, which we are monitoring."

Leesa and Deborah entered the room. The little old man looked feeble under the white sheets.

Michael sat himself up and assessed the new girl. She was fair skinned, like his Charlene. She had her hair wrapped up in a tight bun and very little makeup.

"Mr. Sylva, this is Leesa Barnes, she is joining our staff today," Deborah explained.

Michael grunted a greeting.

"How are you feeling today?" Leesa asked her new patient.

"Much better, Doctor, I think I am ready to go home now. I have some things I have to do."

"She's not a doctor, she is a nurse like me," Deborah's voice was curt.

"Sorry sir, you *are* doing better, but it's best you stay. We have to make sure you are in perfect health before we can let you go home," Leesa's smiled. Deborah wasn't ever one to give a patient false hope. She resented that Lisa would. She gave a quick side-eye glance to show her disapproval. Michael started shaking his head violently. "No, no, there is not time for that! I don't need to be perfect. I have to go say my goodbyes, you don't understand. I have a dress for her!"

Deborah moved in fast to give her patient a shot of sedatives. "He tends to become overwhelmed and has been demanding to go home every day," she explained to Leesa.

Leesa felt sorry for the old man and didn't quite like the care her training nurse had given him.

"I am going to stay with him for a bit," Leesa announced.

'We have many more patients," Deborah was about to demand Leesa accompany her, then realized things would be faster without her tagging along.

"Suit yourself!" Deborah huffed, before walking out of the room.

Montreal

Pierre sat in his kitchen drinking a cup of coffee. He listened to French music. A singer from his country, Cameroon. Tears flowed freely as he listened to the beautiful voice of Simone Nebowi. The music played over the sobs. He could only remember feeling pain like this once before, when his mother died. Now he had no one. He felt alone and broken. His lover had left, and he couldn't imagine how he would go on. She was his world. Pierre and Charlene had travelled together, they cooked and enjoyed dining. Pierre was enchanted by his relationship that defied everything he knew about love. To love a free woman was unheard of. He remembered how strongly his family emphasized being a man, getting a woman and having a family. He didn't do any of it. He didn't blame Charlene. He chose the life she offered. Now he had to live with the lonely consequences. The thought that haunted him most at this time was the memory of leaving her a few years back. He had left her then, and now she was leaving him. In one of her recent episodes with dementia, Charlene sent Pierre away only two weeks ago. He couldn't bear the pain of trying to see her again, so that was the last time he would ever see her. Now she was gone forever. He fell to the floor, reliving the pain.

Pierre sobbed on, remembering that evening when he showed up at the apartment for his regular Sunday night visit. He had brought her flowers, as he often did. Daisies in a simple, wild arrangement. She loved daisies. He handed them to her when he entered. He was talking to Anton while Charlene busied herself in the kitchen. Pierre crept in and kissed her on the back of her neck as he had done many times. Charlene spun around and looked at him as though she had never seen him before. Her eyes intense, her smile absent.

"You need to watch yourself! My husband is a very big man, you don't want to mess with him!" she said. Pierre was first shocked, and then thought to laugh. Charlene has always had such a crazy sense of humour, but she didn't laugh this time. Her face just got sterner.

"Do you make it a habit of coming to people's houses and trying to steal their women? No, not here fella, you need to get your things and leave! We are not having that!" Pierre was shocked. Even Anton had joined them in the kitchen.

"Charlene, Pierre came to see you," Anton explained, his voice gentle like he was speaking with a child.

Charlene shook her head strongly, "I am not going to have a fight here tonight, I am not going to tell you what your friend here just did, but I think he should leave," she was agitated and confused.

Anton could see the disbelief and fear in Pierre's eyes. Pierre had no idea what the past couple of weeks had been like. Anton hoped Charlene was going to be better when she saw her lover. Not only did she seem to have forgotten their love, but she didn't remember that she was a free-loving poly woman. Pierre left the apartment so angry. He didn't know what to do with his feelings. Once in his car, he called Anton. They talked for a while and Anton explained how quickly Charlene was leaving herself. They agreed it was best for Pierre not to come by unless she asked for him. Two weeks later, Charlene died.

Memphis

Marcy cleaned up the mess from the night before. James was still sleeping. She thought about all the things he had said last night. It wasn't in her nature to be sorry or admit she was wrong. "And where has that gotten you?" she could hear her mother's voice in her ear.

Marcy took a seat in the kitchen, propping up her less swollen ankle. She thought about all the good times with James. When they met, and the truly happy times. She had to admit she was the main cause of their break. She always thought it was him who stopped being interested in her, but now she could see that she made it hard to live a happy life. She put demands on him straight after the nuptials, she was judgmental and lived to be right. The very thoughts storming in her mind made her angry.

"Such a fool!" she said out loud. "Such a damn fool," she said, disgusted.

James entered the kitchen as Marcy was in mid-sentence.

'You calling me a fool?" he asked, pouring himself a coffee.

"No, I am a damn fool," she stated.

James was surprised. He never heard Marcy talk like that before. He reached into the cupboard, found another cup and poured his ex-wife a steaming cup of java.

"Now, why you callin' my girl a fool?" he teased.

"Hmph, your girl wasted a lot of our time, didn't she?" Marcy asked. Her face softened with sincerity.

"Life ain't over," he answered. Marcy's eyebrows raised.

"We never did talk about second chances," she said. Marcy hoped she was not projecting or seeing things differently than they were.

"You were angry for a long time. Shit, you were angry and still coming over to take care of me. I would have brought up the topic, but not until you let go of all that." He made a gesture, waving his hand up and down her body.

Marcy sat down at the kitchen table.

"I am 58 years old James. I don't know how much I can change all this," she made the same hand gesture.

"You ain't gotta change it, just some tweaking and refining Marce. I want you to... just think about what's important." He expressed.

She did. Marcy took a moment to think about her life and needs. "Happiness," she whispered.

"Okay and can that happiness be us just enjoying and taking care of each other, or does that happiness have to be you showing everyone the whipped-up nigga you have?" Marcy was shocked by the tone James took, but also wanted to laugh. She seriously thought about the question.

"I would very much like for us to take care of each other, and have fun together," she admitted.

"Are you going to be okay with giving me some space so I can do the things I like without guilt or shaming?" he asked.

Marcy nodded.

"Good! You gonna be okay with me having a booty call from my heavy breasted neighbour Mrs. Thompson?" he asked in the same tone.

"Hell naw! What the..." Marcy laughed loudly. Her own laughter sounded so foreign to both of them.

"Just kidding," James leaned in and kissed Marcy.

"I have a little trip to take, I am going to my friend's memorial and paying respects. When I get back you and I will really, really talk about bringing this all back together," James spoke.

'I can come? I..."

James gave Marcy a look. This changed her thoughts and she re-evaluated.

"Right. Space." Marcy smiled.

James packed his favourite suit into a garment bag, grabbed a few toiletries and left for the airport quite at peace. He asked Marcy to stay at his place and rest her ankle. His thoughts were circling a spectrum of joy, contentment and sadness. Making things up with Marcy felt important to James, but saying farewell to Charlene was also important at this time.

Montreal

Anton and Darrin went to view a few venues while shopping for a place to hold the memorial. The first one was a church basement on the other side of town. They both knew the moment they stepped inside, it was a solid No. Charlene really had no love for churches or religion. Eventually they were lucky to find a veteran's hall not far from the condo. With the hall booked, Anton and Darrin were working hard to get through the to-do list. Sara had found a lot of information online regarding funerals and celebration of life ceremonies. Shelly was great at adding personal things Charlene would want done. The memorial was going to be an all-day event with a special time slot for close friends and family. Anton had been informing people via email. Darrin was in charge of organizing speeches and hiring musicians to play music throughout the day. His mother had so many musician and artist friends. He soon became aware of how many wanted to perform a song or read a piece at the memorial. One woman just cried the whole phone call. The two men became mentally and physically exhausted from the preparations and the grief.

The day was cold and grey. Anton pulled into Tim Horton's and suggested they sit there and hash out the rest of their given tasks. Darrin agreed. The coffee might be shit, but he lived in Europe for the past eight years and could murder someone for a cup of weak Tim's coffee.

Anton looked worn over the past few days. Darrin was concerned for his well-being.

"How bad was it?" he asked, ready to finally have this conversation with his "step-friend".

Anton shook his head. He took a deep breath. Darrin fiddled with the plastic lid of his coffee cup.

"She showed signs of leaving over the past month, everyday more so. She just wasn't there anymore. The first real big one was when she entered the building and stayed at Abdul's desk. She just stood there. After about five minutes, Abdul asked if she needed anything and she just smiled. Then she admitted that she couldn't remember which apartment she lived in. Abdul is such a kind man, he made her feel like it was a common mistake among tenants, and that he was always helping people back to their units. He opened the door for her and let her in and then texted me." Anton explained. I really started to worry. Took a bit of talking before she would even consider going to a doctor."

Darrin could feel the tears rushing to his eyes.

'You didn't call me,' he said.

"No, she would never forgive me if you saw her like that. She was proud of how you saw her, she used to always bring up how you spoke at her fiftieth birthday, that toast you made. She wanted you to always see her like that. She made me promise I wouldn't expose her. Your mother was a warrior of a woman, she didn't deal well with confusion or weakness. It was hard on her. One day she went to the store for paints and came back with a wig. The art store is close to the beauty store, but then that night she tried to finish her painting and started crying." Anton wiped his eyes.

"Well she did love her wigs," Darrin offered. Anton attempted to laugh. He loved Darrin's comedic outlook, but his emotions won and he leaked out a stifled cry.

"Yeah, I took her to the doctor. He said she was moving through the stages very quickly. She lost over 40 percent of memory within weeks. Can you imagine just days, years missing? She would forget you were abroad and ask if you were coming over, or if Shelly was still coming to dance class, then she asked Pierre to leave because she didn't remember they were lovers. Another time, she thought she was getting ready for a bike trip. She actually started packing up her bike's saddle bags. I stayed home more and tried to keep her safe and in good company." Anton gave a big sigh. "It was so hard watching her leave me and yet seeing her beside me," he cried.

The day had been draining on Anton and Darrin. They arrived back at the apartment building to find Sara alone in the darkening afternoon.

"Where did Shelly go?" Darrin asked.

Sara went into the kitchen to reheat her coffee.

"She is gone for a few hours, she said we should cook the food in the refrigerator, but..."

"Don't feel like cooking?" Darrin asked, knowing Sara's mood.

Sara shook her head.

"You stay with Anton. I am going to get us some food. I love the Portuguese chicken from this place not far away, I will be no longer than 40 minutes." With a quick kiss on her forehead, Darrin rushed out into the cold, dark evening.

Anton had made a sandwich and tea. He placed his meal on the table beside his favourite chair and moved towards his records. He slowly searched out a selection.

"Feels like a Lionel Richie night," he smiled at Sara.

The music was good. It was romantic, yet calm. Sara took a seat across from Anton.

'This is nice" she said. Anton nodded and took a bite of his sandwich.

"Darrin went to get chicken, but you don't eat that, I am told."

Anton shook his head while chewing.

'How long have you been vegetarian?" she asked. She had not had a chance to speak with Anton and she had so many questions.

Taking a sip of his tea, Anton thought back through the years.

"About 30 years now," he said.

Sara's eyes widened. "Wow, that is a long time! And your wife, she was a vegetarian, too?"

Anton nodded. "Charlene stopped eating meat when we met, but she would have some fish sometimes. She was very particular about her body, that woman," he mused.

Somehow that bothered Sara. She had been feeling some sort of way about her body as of late. She knew she had gained at least five pounds within the last week. The food in Montreal was as good as Darrin had bragged about over the years.

"She just always needed to be strong for her bike rides," Anton added as if he could sense Sara's feelings.

"Pierre seems nice," Sara blurted out, not knowing how to be subtle about what she wanted to know.

"Pierre is a good man. Charley was quite fond of him."

"He said he was...he was with her for many years, like ten," she stated.

Anton nodded. "Ten...sounds about right. Well, minus the year he left."

This was new information. Sara wondered why Pierre left for a year and then returned.

"He left?" she inquired.

Anton nodded. "Charley's biggest fear in life was that Pierre would leave her." He took another bite of his sandwich, making Sara wait on the gossip piece she wanted to hear.

"Wasn't she worried about you leaving?" she asked.

"Naw, I would never leave her," he said matter-of-factly.

"I am a polyamorous man, with a polyamorous woman. No need to leave. But Pierre wasn't. He was a monogamous man in love with a polyamorous woman. Eventually, monogamous men always want certain things..."

"Like what?" she asked. Sara didn't have a lot of experience with men. Darrin had been her second boyfriend after a six-year relationship.

"Like a wife and family, a home. Usual things," he offered.

Sara let the words sink in. Seems like a normal thing for a normal man to want, she thought to herself.

"He left, but he must have returned? Why?" she asked. "What makes a man come back when he had a plan?"

"He came back." Anton closed his eyes and listened to the music, leaving Sara to her thoughts and knowing she had more questions. The music started to lift Anton's spirits. It always did. He moved his head to the sounds.

Darrin and a greasy bag of chicken blew through the door before Sara had chance to obtain any more details about the Pierre-Charlene saga.

Chapter 6

Boston

The new nurse attending to Michael seemed a heck of a lot nicer than that heifer, Deborah. She actually spoke to him like a grown person. She could also draw blood without abusing his little veins. A tiny smile appeared on Michael's face when he saw Leesa enter his room. She had a big warm smile that started in her eyes and exploded her lips.

"You're looking so much better!" She even smelled nice. Michael was feeling better and his colour had come back. He sat up in his bed and wiped his chin, hoping his appearance wasn't too bad. He was what they called dapper back in his day. Always shaven, clean cut and a bit of jewellery for an added touch.

"Yes, I have to get my release soon," he smiled as Leesa neared his bed.

"Oh, Mr. Sylva, I'm so sorry. You won't be released any time soon. We really need to keep a watch on you. Your liver and kidneys are not working the way we need them to be. You are looking better, but..." she trailed off, reading his chart. Michael's liver was shutting down and his kidneys were next. She knew he was not leaving this hospital alive. The colour in his eyes told her he had a few days left, if not hours.

"But I've got to go, I have things to do!" Michel tried to raise his voice, but he was hardly audible.

"Where is it you're in such a hurry to go, anyway?" she asked sweetly.

Michael remained quiet as he decided whether or not to tell the nice new nurse of his intentions.

"I have to go say goodbye to my friend," he barely whispered. Leesa could feel his pain, and his face spoke of the heaviness he felt.

"Mr. Sylva, your family and friends should be coming here to say goodbye," Leesa informed her patient.

"No, not a goodbye for me, goodbye to her." Michael appeared agitated.

Leesa increased his dosage, hoping he would calm down and rest. It wasn't helping him to be in such a state. She was worried.

"She will understand, you're too sick to go anywhere Mr. Sylva. Maybe you can write a letter." she suggested.

"She can't understand, she is dead." He made his voice work that time. Leesa was shocked.

"Oh, I am sorry."

"That is why I have to go say goodbye to my Carmel muse," he concluded.

Leesa took a seat beside Michael's bed. She knew the sedative would soon kick in and he would be off to sleep. "Did this just happen?" she asked.

Michael reached for his phone on his little table. He brought up a page and handed the phone to Leesa. She began reading it to herself.

"This Charlene Reese, Canadian artist, she was a friend of yours?" she asked.

Michael nodded.

"She was my muse." The words came out slowly, and then he was sleeping. Deborah poked her head through the door.

"You're running late," she barked, before disappearing down the hallway. Leesa put Michaels phone back on his table.

Toronto

Andrea was alone in her apartment. She had gotten the high-rise condo in her divorce. It was three times the size of the little apartment Marlon Styles lived in. She often thought it was much too large of a space for just herself. She poured a large glass of red wine and made herself comfortable in the living room. The news played on the TV in the background. She sat up when a photo of Charlene Reese came onto her screen. Her interest was piqued, so she Googled the woman.

A lot of images and web news of the artist flashed on her screen. Andrea was intrigued. With increasing interest, she looked through the search results. It said Charlene Reese had cycled across Canada at age 50. It showed photos of the artist in her home with her beautiful paintings. There were hundreds of articles and photos of this woman from a young age until her death announcement. The news report stated the memorial in Montreal would be expecting many to grieve the popular artist. Andrea brought up Charlene's Facebook page. It had been flooded with "Rest in Peace" wishes and tributes. She saw pictures of her with friends of all ages and diversities. Charlene Reese was a stunning woman with an interesting life.

That night Andrea followed Charlene down the internet rabbit hole with articles, blogs, YouTube videos, and news clippings. She couldn't get enough of the things this woman had done with her life. She even came across a photo of Charlene and Marlon. They shared the same look of adoration. Charlene Reese was a polyamorous Black woman in a time when no one would consider such a lifestyle, especially a Black woman. She was rebellious and adventurous, well-travelled and creative. It was three in the morning when Andrea finally fell asleep with her laptop still on her leg and Charlene Reese on her mind.

Montreal

Pierre heard the light tapping on his apartment door. He had been just sitting in his little kitchen reminiscing and weeping. He wiped the tears from his eyes and slowly walked to the door. He was very surprised to see

Shelly standing there with a bag that smelled like his favourite chicken dinner. Shelly hugged him as she pushed her way into the apartment. Pierre lived on the French side of town. She could hear a passionate French woman yelling at her husband through the kitchen walls. Pierre turned up his little radio to mute the invasive sounds. Placing the brown paper bag on the counter, Shelly went to refill the kettle while Pierre took his seat by the kitchen window.

"Je t'apporte de la bonne repase (I brought you some food)!" she spoke in French. There had been a few evenings at Charlene's when Shelly would practise her learned French with Pierre. After many years of living in the French city, Shelly could claim to be quite fluent in her French. Unlike Charlene, who struggled with the language. Charlene often relied on Pierre to speak for them in social settings.

Pierre was afraid of his emotions. He had not been dealing well with Charlene's death. Everything seemed to tip him over. A photo, a song and now the smell of food. He looked at the bag on the counter. The grease had begun to discolour the bag,

"She always brought me Portuguese chicken," His voice was soft

"She didn't even eat meat, but she would go across town and get me the best chicken dinner," He pointed towards the counter. "Is it from Da Silvas?" he asked.

Shelly smiled. "Yes, she took me to that little chicken shack years ago. So many years ago, well, when she used to eat meat, that long ago," Shelly smiled.

"Do you want me to make you up a platter?"

Pierre shook his head. He had no appetite. Shelly knew this was going to be hard on him.

"You have to take care of yourself," she frowned, worried about him.

Pierre looked dishevelled and unkempt. He wore his faded blue house coat over a track suit.

"She wouldn't want you to fall apart." Shelly tried to bring up his spirits but couldn't. He was crumbling in front of her. Shelly knew Pierre was holding in all his feelings and trying not to let his composure fail.

"I loved that woman," he cried.

Shelly felt the tears stinging her eyes.

"I know, and she loved you so much, she talked about you all the time. Pierre is taking me to Quebec for the weekend, Pierre is learning to tap dance, Pierre is buying a new car, she told me so much about you. She adored you." Shelly sat close to her friend.

Pierre wiped his face again.

"I know she did, she ...had this way of making you feel like you were a king, the only man in the world, and I was neither, but when I was with her, it was just a man and a woman in love."

Shelly got up and busied herself. She made two cups of tea and smiled, knowing it was Charlene's favourite brand of tea. Then she started fixing him a plate. Shelly placed the plate on the table. She knew he wouldn't eat, but maybe later he might. She could feel Pierre's pain. He was so alone. He didn't have anyone else in Canada. Charlene was his world.

Pierre leaned back in his chair. He was happy to be able to talk about his lover. His loneliness was taking over him since her death. He sipped his tea and looked into Shelly's big, kind eyes.

"The very first night I shared with her, she was in my bed, we had made love and, oh, she was beautiful. I was so taken, I wanted to know everything about this goddess of a woman. I knew about Anton and their relationship, and I was nervous. I didn't know what she wanted of me or how it was going to work. I knew she was polyamorous but I don't think I understood what it meant until that night, in the dim lit room, she looked at me and said, "Pierre, 'polyamorous' means I can love more than one person, which I believe we all can and do. It also means that no matter what just happened in this bed with you, it doesn't change my love or relationship with Anton, and what Anton and I have doesn't stop me from falling in love with you. I feel everything I would feel if I didn't have a lover already, and more because we share an honesty that few people readily know how to handle." Pierre let the words linger. Many nights had been shared with Pierre, Vern, Anton and Shelly hashing over love and romance at Charlene's. He knew Shelly was well versed on Charlene's views.

"She taught me so much about love, and I know how great her life was. And I know I had almost eleven beautiful years with her. But I can't stop this pain, this feeling of not having more, or enough. I should have made more time, or followed her on some of her rides, I should have..." the words fell into soft sobs.

"I know," said Shelly, "I can't stop thinking about her and all the times we all shared. I think the one thing that will always haunt my perfect memories of Charlene, would be the day I told her I was engaged. She was so happy for me and we celebrated with a cake from the bakery across the street. Charlene was so proud of me and she beamed and then…" Shelly's face clouded over; her eyes swelled with the threat of more tears.

Pierre remembered the situation Shelly was speaking of.

"Char was so happy for me and Vern. She liked him immediately and he liked her. She just got so excited about it. I was surprised because she had no intentions of ever marrying, yet she was elated when I told her he proposed. She started talking about the dress. We talked about styles and cuts. She asked if it was going to be in a church. We just talked like, well, like the friends that we were. She was Charlene, full of life and ready to plan things. Then she asked so innocently if she could have both you and Anton on her invite. I was so stupid. I just didn't handle it well. I had known you for many years. And Anton, well I lived with them. Anton and I are really close. I adore you both, like uncles. In my head it made sense. Of course, Char would want you both there. You both mean so very much to her. And to me, to be honest. But for the first time, I just couldn't. I thought about Vern's Haitian mother and French father and their values and how people would talk. I was torn and really struggled with it. I didn't talk to Charlene for weeks. I didn't know what to say or do. I cried over it, thinking how shallow I was being and that I wasn't showing her the love or openness she had always given me." Shelly wept thinking about it.

Shelly wiped her eyes, glad the box of tissues was available. She had not been able to freely cry since hearing about Charlene's death.

"She knew that was hard for you," Pierre consoled her.

"I… I almost made her have to choose which of you could come and it broke my heart. "she sniffled.

"You made the best choice in the end." He pointed to a photo held by a magnet on his fridge.

It was Shelly in her beautiful brides dress with Charlene, Anton and Pierre.

Shelly looked at it, wiped her tears, and found a small smile.

"It was Vern. He saw me crying with her invitation in front of me. It said, 'Charlene Reese plus one'. And he just grabbed a pen and wrote 'plus one more'. He said it would all be fine, and it was," she cried.

"It was," Pierre agreed. He held Shelly until her crying ceased.

"I came here to console you," she muttered.

"You did," Pierre smiled.

"I am so glad you came to see me. I don't know what I am going to do with all these feelings. I cried. I went to the apartment. Seeing this young man who is the very image of Charlene, it made me want to weep more. It is hard. Many people cannot understand the complexity of these relationships. I loved this woman. I had since we met. You have a time of regret and I have a huge regret, too, that causes me so much pain whenever I think about it."

Pierre reached for the tissue, also.

"We were so happy, and everything was just fine, and then I made a horrible choice after your wedding."

Shelly nodded. She remembered the day Charlene told her. After her two-week honeymoon in Saint Barth's.

On a warm spring afternoon in Montreal, the terraces on Crescent street were crowded. Shelly and Charlene found a small table at the end of the sidewalk.

"You look beautiful! Marriage suits you," Charlene said to Shelly, who was well tanned and looking quite refreshed from her holiday.

"We had too much fun!" Shelly whipped out her phone and scrolled through the many photos of her honeymoon.

"It was amazing! I am so happy, and I meant to tell you it was so great having the three of you at my wedding," Shelly smiled.

Charlene tried to smile, but her face couldn't quite make it work.

The waitress put both of their drinks down, and Shelly waited until she was out of hearing range.

"What's wrong?" Shelly demanded.

Charlene tried again to find an expression closer to a smile.

"He left," her tone was soft. Charlene bit down on her lip. "Pierre left. He met a woman. He decided to start a family and settle down, which we all knew could happen and...it did."

Shelly was shocked. He was always so smitten with Charlene when they were together, but she also understood he wanted children and was younger than Charlene.

"Are you okay?" she asked.

Charlene nodded and went into her "warrior goddess" mode. Being strong was always Charlene's way.

"Yep," she sipped her drink and demanded to see more beach photos.

"She was devastated when you left," Shelly remembered. Charlene had been lost for months after Pierre left. Anton would ask Shelly to take her out and try to cheer her up.

"I know," he nodded.

"I wanted a child, and I met a woman who promised she would give me this. But I would have to be in a traditional relationship. She wasn't having the 'sharing' thing. She had many not-so-good words to say about Charlene's lifestyle. Anyway, after one year, nothing was moving in the direction of the plan. She was making me crazy, angry, and taking all the money I worked for. Still no baby, no love, no happiness, which I think might have been ok if I had not known Charlene already. I would not have known this happiness. I thought about it. Just because I made a big mistake, doesn't mean I could not fix this. So, I did. Et voila, I returned to my love. My forgiving, open-loving woman. She took me back and we continued," he smiled.

Shelly smiled too. "We were lucky to have her in our lives".

Charlotte

Helen returned home form a long shift at the clinic. She was looking forward to spending some time with her oldest son, maybe taking her father and son out for dinner. They both loved Applebee's. The house seemed so quiet when she entered, which was strange. Usually, she found Kevin playing video games in front of the television. She placed her purse on the kitchen table and grabbed a glass from the cupboard. A cold glass of pink grapefruit juice was calling to her. Before she could open the refrigerator door, the note held in place by her Puerto Rico magnet caught her eye. Snatching it off, she read it out loud.

"Granddad and I are going on a little trip. Will be back in a couple days. Love you."

The note was in Kevin's hard to read handwriting.

"What the hell," She cursed, tossing the note in the kitchen trash can.

"Now, where in the world are those two going?" Helen wondered out loud, as she pulled out her empty carton of juice. The carton followed Kevin's note as Helen grabbed her keys and took herself to Applebee's.

Nassau

Shirley had cleaned up the emptied bottles from the night before. They were among the last evidence of the many drinks consumed by her and Dory throughout the evening. Dory had passed out sprawled on the living room sofa. Shirley logged on to her computer while Dory slept. Posts of 'rest in peace' and other tributes were still coming in on Charlene's page. Photos of Charlene and many people were surfacing.

"She really was a popular woman," Shirley thought as she clicked through some photos. Charlene posed with an older white man with their packed bikes in front of them. Some old dance photos, even a few of her with her son traveling. The whistling of the kettle woke Dory from her heavy slumber.

Dory was startled as she processed her surroundings. Memories were flashing through her thoughts.

"Coffee?" Shirley offered.

"Tea, please," 'Dorey mumbled. "Oh, my head…" Dorey staggered to the downstairs bathroom.

A steamy hot cup of tea was placed where the wine glasses from the previous night still lingered.

"Well, you handled the bender quite well," Dory teased.

'Yup. Got lots done. Cleaned the house, took out the trash, made some calls, and bought two plane tickets to Canada!"

Dory sipped her drink, letting each word slowly translate through her fog.

"Plane tickets? Two? Canada? What?" Dory asked, shocked.

"Montreal, I am going to Charlene's memorial. I spoke with her... husband? Anton. We leave early tomorrow morning," Shirley grinned.

"Are you serious?" Dory couldn't believe the words her friend was speaking.

"You are going to Montreal, to another woman's funeral, just like that? Just fly across the water and show up?" Dory snapped her finger for effect.

"Nope, WE are going." Shirley gleamed.

Dory quickly went from serious and concerned to overjoyed.

"We're going to Montreal?" she shrieked.

Shirley nodded.

"I guess I need to go home and get my things together." Dory pushed her tea away as she tried to get up from the kitchen island.

"Come back tonight. We leave for the airport at 5 a.m."

"5 a.m.," Dory shouted, letting her smile die. She mumbled many more words before getting to the door. "Alright," she let herself out the back door. "But we are going to shop right?" she asked, half-jokingly.

"Yes," Shirley confirmed, shutting the door behind Dorey. "Course we will shop," she laughed, latching the door behind her friend.

Chapter 7

Toronto

Marlon boarded the Mega Bus and took a seat on the lower level of the double-decker transit bound for Montreal. The bus filled up quickly. Most of the passengers headed to the top level. Marlon was happy to have a two-seater all to himself. He planned on stretching out and hopefully falling asleep for the next six-and-a-half hours. He tucked his winter coat under his chair and settled in. Traveling had sure changed from his glory days. He used to fly into cities and had been received by limos. Those days were well behind him now. He looked across at the Trinidadian looking lady seated with her grandchild and the African woman behind his chair. No one even recognized him anymore. He was just an old Black man on a bus now.

When the doors closed, he reached for his ear buds. Some sweet R&B would be just the sedative he needed. He could dream about the beautiful times he had with his love, Charlene. The night they danced in a little club in old Montreal.

"This seat taken?" He heard a lady ask. Marlon didn't even want to look up, he tried to think of something to say. Something that would make her not want to sit next to him. Maybe she didn't know about the upper deck. He would just suggest seating up there, he decided to tell the late-boarding passenger.

When Marlon looked up the words died in his mouth. Andrea had been standing over his seat looking like an angel. Marlon smiled, moving his bag from the seat beside him.

His grin told Andrea she did make the right decision. She had been nervous about joining him uninvited, but now she felt great settling in the seat beside the old crooner.

"I have an uncle in Montreal, think I may visit him," she grinned.

Montreal

It took Shelly four hours to mass print all the images they had selected. The photos were all stacked in office boxes which Abdul helped her carry back up to the apartment. Sara was the only one home when she arrived.

"These are all the photos?" Sara opened the box Abdul had left in the hall. The sheer volume was overwhelming.

"So much life!" Sara said, thumbing through the top of the pile.

"Yeah, it's going to take hours to put them up in the hall. But I want all her beautiful moments to be what people see everywhere." Shelly was focused on her idea. She had done so much work in the last couple of days.

"Wow, you are going to need a team!" Sara tossed the stack of photos back in the box.

Shelly went into management mode. "You're right!" She reached for her phone and started scrolling.

This little woman is a machine, Sara thought.

Shelly made sure the boxes were safely tucked away in Charlene's nook. She sat in Anton's chair to rest.

"Where are they guys?" She asked. Sara couldn't remember the many places they said they had to go.

"They are taking care of funeral things," Shelly offered. Sara nodded, pretending to understand. "You didn't want to go with them?" Asked Shelly.

'It's too cold out there," Sara pointed to the balcony. It was a regular winter day. But if one was not used to Canadian winters, it could be considered brutal. Shelly felt bad Sara had just been in the apartment by herself all day.

"I did most of the things on my list, just have to go pay the caterers. If you like, I can get you one of Charlene's winter coats and we can go downtown. I think they have it set up for the winter carnival at Place des Arts."

Sara thought about it. "'Yes, I would like that' she answered.

On the Road

Kevin had the back seat of his granddad's old PT Cruiser filled with junk food. Big Gatorade bottles, bags of chips and store-bought baked goods. He was not happy about the long car ride ahead. He did look forward to spending time with his granddad.

"You sure you got enough?" Ash teased, getting into the driver's seat.

"Granddad, it is a sixteen-hour drive!" Kevin said one more time.

"It's not that bad, we will stop over at your uncle Buddy's in New York, sleep a few hours and continue on." Buddy was Ash's younger brother. He lived just outside of New York city. Kevin adjusted the online radio to sync with his playlist.

"Don't you play none of that vulgar rap stuff, "Ash warned.

"Granddad, I got you. I made this playlist just for you." Kevin turned up the volume. The first song to play was Marvin Gaye.

Ash nodded his head and smiled. His grandson really got him.

Ash clicked on his seat belt, took a sip of his road coffee and watched as his home state was a blur in the rear-view mirror. The drive was long, but Kevin chimed in with a few campus stories and the music selection kept Ash feeling good.

Boston

Leesa returned to see Michael after her shift ended. He was sitting up on his bed listening to music from his phone. He tried to sing along with the song, only getting every third word or so out with his tiny voice. He seemed at peace.

"Other nurse said I could play it low, like this," he said, patting his cell phone lightly.

"Sounds good. That was one of my mother's favourite songs." Leesa smiled at her patient.

"Was?" his expression turned to empathy.

Imagine a man with so little time, feeling compassion about the loss of a stranger. Leesa was touched.

"Yeah, my ma didn't live as long as you have. She died when I was just 15. I miss her a lot," Leesa admitted. Leesa checked the machines and monitors.

There was a moment when only the singer had a voice. Leesa pulled up a chair close to Michael. She could see the glossiness of his eyes. He didn't have much time. She felt bad knowing he was so close to his life's end.

"You still thinking about your friend?" she asked.

Michael's breathing sounded heavy and wet as he tried to speak.

"Charlene Reese was my muse," he said with many breaths padding his words.

"She was a beautiful woman. I got to be in her company a few times." He turned down the volume of the phone. "I was in the clothing industry all my life. I first saw her so many years ago, somehow, I forget…online, maybe one of those first social sites? You know, before Facebook and everything. I saw her. She was just a beautiful, 'red bone' girl," he coughed a smile. "Lena, I decided to call her. She said no one called her that but me. She was a star, like the great Lena Horne. She had a body like a goddess, she looked fabulous in everything. I sent her clothes, new designs from Paris, New York…she was my little unknow star. I thought one day she would get old and maybe not want to wear these cloths no more, maybe get married like women do. But she was still a beautiful muse well into her sixties. You always wait for someone to say, 'I can't be your star anymore, I am getting married, or too old,'" he laughed. "Lena was in it for the long run. She stayed desirable well into her sixties, can you imagine?" Michael needed to place the oxygen mask over his face to continue talking. He wanted to pass this story on to bring life to Charlene once more before he left. Leesa could feel his need to speak and waited by his bed for him to regain strength.

"We went to Vegas once, just us. I brought her a whole suitcase full of clothes, shoes, boots, and even lingerie. She put it all on, sent me photos from her adventures, sometimes wearing my stuff. She was so fun. She entertained me for over thirty years," he confessed.

Leesa held Michael's hand. He had no strength left. He tried to squeeze it, but this made him cough uncontrollably. Leesa quickly ran out of the room to get Mister Sylva more meds. When she returned, his vitals were very low. With a few more shallow breaths, Michael Sylva said good night to his Carmel muse, and bade the world goodbye.

Montreal

Sara enjoyed the outing with her new friend Shelly. Shelly was more relaxed when not consumed with funeral duties. She drove them to the downtown arts district. A winter carnival had been set up there. Shelly was a great guide as she translated things and showed Sara the better things in the city. The two settled on log benches in front of a makeshift fireplace. Sara had bought them both cups of Quebec's mulled wine.

'I had this in Quebec City, you should get Darrin to take you there before you guys return to Holland' Shelly said.

"Oh, the old place, with the castle. I see pictures of this, and the hotel of ice,"

"Yes, that is not far, I spent two nights there with Vern, about five years ago. It's expensive, but amazing. They make this beautiful hotel of ice then it just melts and disappears in spring."

"This sounds good," Sara was happy, she smiled and laughed. They both became aware of how gloomy things had been.

"I'm sorry this is not the best way to visit Canada. But if you come back, I am sure you will love it," Shelly smiled.

Sara nodded. "I do like it, when I am not frozen," she laughed.

Shelly smiled. No one ever gets used to the cold. You just deal with it.

"Charlene used to say, 'it's going to be cold, so just buy yourself some ice skates and ride it out,'"

"You will want to see the mountain too," Shelly added. "They ice skate there in winter."

On the Road

The drive from North Carolina to New York was easy. Just before reaching Buddy's house, a light snow started to fall. They rounded the subdivision and pulled up to the house. "You have arrived at your destination," the GPS lady stated.

Ash and Kevin waited for Buddy to open the door. Kevin bolted in after a quick "Hi uncle! I need to use your washroom." Buddy and Ash laughed as they greeted each other. Ash's younger brother Buddy lived alone. He had never married, and seemed quite happy with his two cats and large TV. Buddy was happy to see Ash, and more so to see his grandnephew Kevin.

A confirmed bachelor, Buddy lived with two cats and a weird collection of toy army figures. Kevin remembered seeing the large collection as a child and was thrilled to see how it had expanded over the years. He came out of the bathroom and grabbed a seat on the sofa. He opened a bag of his chips and made himself comfortable while the old guys caught up at the kitchen table. A mangy looking orange cat made a home at his feet while he surfed channels. The other one was on its owner's lap while the two men talked.

"So, you really crossing the border to Canada? Damn. You know, I have never been there. I don't even have a passport. Shit, I never went anywhere but Florida once," Buddy admitted to his brother.

'Yeah, this is my first time going to Canada. But I've been out of the Country. Been to Jamaica and Cuba. I did that as soon as we were allowed to travel there," Ash added.

"You said something about a funeral. One of them drivers?" Buddy asked.

Ash shook his head. "No, a lady friend." A small hint of a smile pushed on Ash's face. He had never spoken of Charlene to anyone before.

Kevin lowered the volume of his show slightly so he could hear the conversation coming from the kitchen. His granddad had not told him much about the departed woman to whom they were crossing borders to say goodbye.

"Oh, you were stepping out with one of them northern gals!" Buddy teased.

"For years, on and off. Many years…" Ash smiled.

"Really, some women get ya like that!" They both laughed.

Kevin had lowered the volume down too low to even hear the program and listened on.

"If ya gonna have your nose all up in this, might as well join us!" Ash said loudly

Kevin inched the cat off his feet and walked into the small kitchen. He put his Gatorade on the table and pulled up a chair. In the moment, he felt like a man getting ready to talk men's talk.

"Thought you didn't want to talk about her," he mumbled.

"We going to her memorial. I think you should know," Ash retorted.

"Know what?" Both Kevin and Buddy asked in unison.

"The lady, who has left this world, was a very special, wonderful woman. She was my lover for many years. I thought the world of her," Ash began.

"She was married?" Kevin's tone sounded disappointed. More for his grandfather's feelings than any kind of moral issue.

"Nope. Charlene never married. Because she was not like any other woman. She didn't want to marry a man and live out her life fulfilling other people's generic dreams. That's how she put it anyhow."

"Generic dreams," Kevin repeated the words. He understood both words but not how they related to the conversation.

"Pre-fabricated, cookie cutter lifestyles, the marriage, children and the 'stick-to-itiveness', wasn't for her. Charlene had many lovers. I don't know how many or for how long they stayed in her life, but she wasn't ever going to commit to any one person. Well not in the traditional way. I accepted this. She lived in another country. That meant I would see her whenever I could and she'd keep me company. I have had one wife and many girlfriends over the years, and when things finish, that is it. They don't call me on my birthday, they don't check on me when I have an angina attack, nothing. But Charlene has always been there. Checking in, sending pictures, lifting my spirits when I am down, celebrating my wins, even asking about my family," Ash said.

"For how long?" Kevin asked.

Ash smiled, "For about 20 years now. She was with me for so many years." He could see her face and her smile in his mind. He remembered her laugh most. Charlene sure loved to laugh. She had such a healthy sense of humour and playfulness to her.

"I knew her before she met Anton, he is her main guy, they live together," he went on.

"And he knew about you, and the others?" Buddy asked, placing the cat on the floor and grabbing himself another beer.

"Yeah, he knew. He is the one who called me and invited me to the memorial."

Both Buddy and Kevin were shocked. They shared a look and their eyebrows raised.

"I am surprised, granddad. I mean, you always talk about the Christian way and a man taking a wife forever, that's what you taught me and my brother."

The room got quiet as Ash reflected on his own thoughts and beliefs.

"I was teaching you what my dad and his dad taught me about being a man and taking a woman. I guess I was trying to keep old ideas alive somehow, but the more I talked with her, the more I wondered why. We just always did what we've always done. She was the first woman, the first damn person, I ever met who lived this way, and she wasn't trying to push her values on me. She knew I was a man of belief, a country man, and she was big city and 'woke', like a real progressive. I never questioned things until I met her, because most of the people I knew lived the same. I thought that was what I was supposed to do. In the end, I was just happy she wanted to be around an old Country boy like me. We continued on the way we always had, even if it hadn't been working for a long time. I was too old, too set in my ways to openly be like Charlene or Anton, but just being with her was my tiny way of rebelling." He paused for emphasis.

"I couldn't talk to you and your brother or even you, Buddy, about such things. Can you imagine your mother? She would take a piece off me if I started going against what our whole 'culture' had taught us about love and relations. You will see when we get there." He said, looking at Kevin.

"I was just living my life and one day she sent me a message on social media saying she was in Charlotte and heading to Atlanta. She was always on the go. I was so excited. I met with her. She had gotten herself booked in a motel, one out there off the freeway, so I said I could talk. I just wanted a simple life, not to go against the grain. But Charlene, she was the real rebel. She didn't let anything stop her from living the life she wanted. She was breaking all the rules and enjoying herself doing it. So I guess I wanted you, Kevin, to come with me on this trip because I thought you might learn something that might help towards your future happiness. I may not be able to teach a new dog, but I can lead him to water."

The three laughed at the mixed up saying.

"That's real, granddad," Kevin was taking in the openness his grandfather was sharing. He saw his granddad in a different light now.

"I saw her last a few years back. I was going to this conference in Los Angeles. I asked her to come and spend the four days with me. We had so much fun. She was a fun lady..." Ash could feel the tears starting to well up.

Buddy finished his beer. "Sure wish I had a passport," he mused.

"This ain't the Wiz!" Ash joked.

They laughed more and enjoyed the night of sharing tales. Kevin finished off his stash of treats listening to the old guys talk.

Bus Ride

The two-story Mega Bus moved steadily through the frozen highway from Toronto to Montreal. Marlon and Andrea sat in the lower level with a small table between them. Marlon was happy to have a companion on this journey. Andrea had been a life saver through all this. It was hard to imagine they had been strangers only a few days ago.

Marlon enjoyed his view, a beautiful young woman in front of him and beautiful snow-capped scenery outside the large windows around him. For that moment, he could forget the deep pain that had been attacking his heart. He didn't have to think about the sadness he was moving 100 kilometres an hour towards.

Marlon pulled out his travel thermos. He had poured himself a Moroccan tea with entirely too much sugar in it. Sipping on his still hot drink, a little smile was forming. He offered Andrea at a drink from the little top of the thermos. They both settled in with the hot beverage in front of them.

"I used to take this bus to Montreal a lot back in the day. I had a standing gig at Le Balcon," he said.

"That's when you met her?" Andrea asked.

"That is when I reconnected with her," Marlon put his travel mug down.

"I met Charlene way before that. I first met her when I was just 20 years old, and she was 19. I was singing with one of my many, many bands. So many bands. Can't even remember the name of our group!" he chuckled.

The sound of his deep laughter caught the attention of an older Black lady in the seat behind him. She leaned forward to get a view of the man talking. She recognized the singer immediately. She had a hard time pulling herself away from the conversation he was having with the pretty young woman next to him. A woman entirely too young for him.

"But I remember her. She was, uh, the keyboard player's wife's little sister. She walked in the club and my heart, oh my heart raced. She was sweet and cute, but she just looked at me like I was a deviant musician!" He laughed loudly.

"So not love at first sight for her," Andrea pressed.

A signature Caribbean sound seeped through Marlon's teeth. Andrea laughed. She had heard her Jamaican grandmother make the exact sound many times.

"Charlene never paid me no mind until a good 25 years later," he laughed. "She had me so deep in the friend zone!" He shook his head. A few known Jamaican curses were muttered from Marlon.

"Every time I saw her, in every city, I tried. And she would flat out shut me down. She was too busy, had a man, raising her son, lived too far. Too far? I would have moved anywhere," he sighed.

Andrea was shocked at this information. 25 years was a long time. She herself was only 34 years old.

"But would you have?" Andrea challenged.

Marlon thought and slowly shook his head. "Probably not. It's easy to say all this now, to declare such undying love when she is not here. But the truth. Oh, the truth. I was in love with her and by the time she even lifted her head to see me, I sabotaged everything." He became serious, the Caribbean accent faded now.

"She was 45 when you got together." Andrea did some quick mental math.

He made the pulling of air through his teeth sound again.

This sound caught the attention of the small Trinidadian woman in the seat across the aisle from them. If she were a canine, you would have seen her ears stand up. The romance story the old timer was speaking of piqued her interest.

"Got together, if you can call it that. Charlene and I were over before we started. I, please excuse my language, fucked that up in Marlon Styles' record time." The African woman behind him raised her eyebrows, looking forward at the Trinidadian lady who pursed her lips. It seemed many were ready for a story of love. They settled back into their seats for the tale to be told.

"Charlene. If she was indeed the love of my life, I never recovered from what went down between her and I." There was a silence between them when a small voice from across Andrea's chair spoke up.

"Wha' 'appin?" The Trini lady asked from across the aisle.

Andrea, surprised, let out a big laugh and Marlon, not wanting to embarrass the nosy woman, continued to speak. Marlon didn't seem to mind the audience. He was, after all, an entertainer.

"Every time I would see her, I would be so excited. I kept trying. I would say, 'Charlene, can I tell you something?' and she would just be sweet and put me off. She would say 'Marlon, I know you like me,' but there was always a 'but'. 'We live in different cities, you dated a friend, I have a boyfriend.' This went on for years. If she ever tried to use me having a girlfriend as an excuse, I would have told her, I would leave any woman for her, I swear. Then finally, one day she saw that I was performing in Montreal, and I got a message from her on the computer. I thought she was just going to ask for free tickets, but to my utter surprise and delight, she asked if she could be my date for my show. I was over the moon. I danced when I read that message. I answered so quickly. I said I would meet her at the club, and we could go somewhere after if she wanted. I was finally going on a date with Charlene Reese." Marlon flashed all his pearly whites at the memory of it.

Andrea smiled. She could see the younger version of Marlon. His old videos were still online, and Andrea had viewed a few. He was definitely a playa. Good looking, dark ebony skin tone, with a golden voice that dropped panties.

"That evening she came into the club and hid in the back. I couldn't see her, but every once in a while, I would catch a glimpse of her. Her wild and big hair, her shiny black shoes, the movement of her dress. She was quite a looker when she was young, and even more so as she aged. I couldn't wait to finish the first set and run over to her. Felt like the longest set of my life." His face took on his energy.

"When I jumped off stage, I remember introducing her to the band like she was my girl. It was my dream for Charlene to be mine. I had wanted to marry her for a long time. So, after the gig, we went to downtown Montreal. She was just new in town at the time, so I showed her the few places I knew. We went into this small venue I liked. I knew the guys playing there. They treated me like a celeb. I think she was impressed. I got us some drinks and we danced. I held her in my arms, finally, and I breathed in her scent. Felt the warmth from her neck, then she looked up at me and kissed me." He drew in a deep breath.

"I was in heaven. The world just became perfect. Marlon Styles was living his dream. Best night of my life. We danced, went back to her place, talked all night long, made out like teenagers. I poured my heart out to this woman, like it was my last and only chance. I told her everything, my intentions, my life dreams. Where I saw her in my life," he conveyed.

The women seated behind and across from Marlon were now openly paying attention to his story. One of them had even begun to eat from a large bag of Popcorn.

"She was listening to everything I was saying, so warm and loving. I said, 'Charlene, I want to be your man. I have wanted to be with you forever.' You know what she said?" he asked Andrea directly, looking her straight in the eyes.

"No?" Andrea answered with sadness.

"No, she said yes! After all those years, Charlene said yes to me!" He pounded the table to make a point.

"I came back to Toronto knowing Charlene Reese was my lady. We talked on the phone, sent photos, connected through every kind of social media. I was spinning with happiness. I figured on my next trip to Montreal, we could talk about how to see each other more often. I was open to whatever. I would come every other week, she could bus to Toronto on Holidays. I knew I wanted that woman as my wife. It was the happiest I had ever been. It was my dream come true," he confessed.

"What happened?" Andrea could feel the build-up and suspected sadness was about to explode. She already knew the ending.

"I didn't make it back for about two months. Then I came to perform for New Year's. I spent three days with her, making love, talking, laughing. I met her son. It was special. Then, on the fourth day, when I left for the bar, she stayed behind with her boy. I didn't return that night. I didn't see her again for six months."

"You didn't return? You left for the gig and...?" Andrea was perplexed.

"I didn't return. I left; I went to sing."

Andrea stared at him. He couldn't look at her.

The woman in the back seat couldn't make out what the silence meant.

"The next time I saw Charlene, she was a different woman. I don't know if I broke something inside of her or awoke something, but my chances with that woman were gone forever. My chance of marriage, anyway," he said.

"Wait. Back up. I don't understand. What happened that night?" Andrea asked.

The Trini lady nodded. She wanted answers too.

"What do you think?" his voice was small.

Andrea just stared.

The silence was stretched.

"You cheated on dat girl!" A voice from the back seat spoke. The elderly African woman nodded knowingly.

"It took six months before I could admit that to her," he said shamefully.

"I wanted and needed her to believe the garbage I was telling her, but she knew. She knew what she knew, that I was never good enough, and I knew." He took in a huge breath, tears filling up his eyes, a plea in his voice.

"So that was it. The small but significant relationship," Andrea said. She seemed disappointed, and knew there had to be more than just fleeting romance and a bad start.

Marlon opened his eyes wide. The tears were rushing freely down his withered face.

"Oh no, that's not it. That was just the beginning," he confessed.

Again, he had everyone's attention. Marlon finished his drink.

"The next time I laid eyes on Charlene, she was the most changed woman I have ever met. She said things to me I couldn't understand, and she did it with love in her eyes and a man at her side."

"Wait, what?" Andrea was completely intrigued.

In Flight

Their flight was six hours long with a changeover in Toronto. Dory settled into her window seat and ordered a gin and tonic straight away. Shirley decided that she would keep herself straight and just had a soda water.

"I still can't believe we are flying across waters to attend your dead husband's ex-girlfriend's funeral," Dory said after her second drink turned empty.

Shirley laughed. "Well it's the least I can do, she flew across the water to say farewell to Derrick."

This was new information to Dory. "Wait, when? Was she at his funeral?" Dory tried to remember that day. It wasn't a large gathering. She knew most of the people there. They were mostly Island folk.

"After," Shirley said. At this moment, the air hostess was picking up Dory's plastic cup.

"Can we have two more of those?" asked Dory. Shirley didn't protest.

"She showed up in Nassau one week after the funeral. Came to my house, just showed up. I came home from work, my first day back and she was on my doorstep holding a bottle of whiskey," Shirley explained.

"No." Dory's voice was loud, but thankfully muffled by the airplane sounds.

"I was shocked, but I was also...not shocked. It was Charlene, she was...different. I wondered about her after the funeral, if she was going to come or not. Then I forgot about it, and when I saw her on the doorstep, it felt like a friend coming to help me close the door and move forward. You know when he died, I was so lost. I just couldn't cope. And I didn't want you, or my daughter, or anyone else to see how hurt I was. But when Charlene came, I knew she loved and adored Derrick and it just seemed right."

Dory nodded. She had learned more about her friend in the past few days than she had in their whole 12-year friendship.

"So, she just came to...talk?" Dory asked.

"She came to have a drink, to Derrick and his life. She sat up in my kitchen and she put the bottle on the table and reached into her little purse and pulled out a shot glass. It had the word 'Forever' written on it. I knew what she was doing. I grabbed a shot glass and we finished that bottle. We talked about Derrick. We laughed, we cried, we bonded. Charlene Reese left my place sometime in the earliest hours of morning. I got a message on my computer saying bye, and she was gone. And now, never to be seen again. So, I am going to Montreal to meet her husband and to share a drink to her. I know you think that is crazy, but it's just something I have to do," Shirley stated. She hoped that Dory didn't think she was crazy.

Boston

Leesa had taken Michael Sylva's little suitcase with his belongings to be disposed of. She felt terrible about her patient who had no one to visit him, care about him or collect is belongings. She looked through the bag. He had an old photograph, it looked like it was ripped from a magazine, of the great actress Lena Horne. He had two lacey pairs of black panties and a white silk pair of gloves. Wrapped up in white paper was a small hand-made gift that caught her attention. Quickly she shoved the items in the front pocket of her floral scrubs before tossing the case into the bin for disposal.

After her shift, Leesa found herself searching random words in the computer. In no time, she had images of Charlene Reese. Her art, dance shows and testimonies from people in the polyamorous circles. With every click of the mouse, Leesa found herself at sites and blogs from all over the world. It was 3 a.m. when Leesa fell asleep at her desk, dreams of Michael's muse swimming in her head. Leesa had never even heard of polyamory before. Wild images of a woman with men all around her invaded her sleep.

Memphis

James's flight was slightly delayed. He had already been to the bar lounge and finished a whiskey sour and a beer. He made himself comfortable in the boarding area. He thought about the time he and Reesy went to Newfoundland, and the times she came to visit Memphis. He was going to miss this fantastic woman, but was more grateful he was able to know her. A musical sound from his phone snapped him out of his nostalgia. It was a photo message from Marcy. He braced himself, hoping it wasn't a photo of her bruised leg. It was not. A roar of laughter bellowed through the airport as James tried to pull himself together. Marcy had sent him a rather racy photo of herself. Naked in his bed wearing shoes he couldn't believe she owned. His laughter roared throughout the waiting area surrounding his gate in the airport. James laughed himself onto the plane. Marcy had made the travel much more interesting. The two texted like school kids until his flight lifted off.

Chapter 8

Ash and Kevin had crossed the border without a problem and only had an hour left before they were in the city of Montreal. Kevin was wide awake, taking in the view.

"So, you booked us in an Airbnb, granddad?" he asked.

"Yeah," Ash said, tapping the GPS device. The clock in the car had changed the time ahead to fit the current time zone.

It was already getting dark as they entered the city.

"Is it downtown, like around clubs and things?" his grandson asked.

"The ad says close to downtown. It is not far from the place I am going, which is why I booked it," Ash answered.

"I know. It's just, I would like to have a little fun on this trip. I heard Montreal is famous for strip clubs!" Kevin joked.

Ash looked from the road to his grandson.

The city unfolded beautifully after they crossed a couple of bridges. Kevin was impressed as they navigated through neighbourhoods heading for their accommodations.

"Look at all these houses. They all have fire escapes, nice." Kevin was truly loving the old French architecture when Ash pulled over outside a beautiful three-story house.

"This is it, 2645," Ash pointed to the house. The quaint, brick house on the quiet street suited Ash just fine. It looked just like the photo from the site, he thought, as he reached into the back seat for his travel bag.

Kevin grabbed his own bag and headed for the front door.

"No, that is 2643. Up there." Ash pointed up the stairs to the second level. Kevin looked up and then around the side of the house.

"Up there? We have to walk up the stairs?" he asked, hoping there was another option.

"How else would we get in?" his grandfather teased. The two men walk up the long staircase to the front door. Ash opened it to find another set of stairs inside.

"Hell! I hate Montreal houses," he could hear Kevin mumble behind him.

On the Bus

Marlon had Andrea's full attention now. The bus had stopped for a change of drivers in Kingston and Andrea rushed out to grab two hot teas for the second part of their ride to Montreal. Once the bus had pulled out of the station, she looked at Marlon to continue his story.

"The next time I saw her was about six months later. She knew I cheated and... well, I did what men do. I refused to admit it. Then finally I knew I had to come clean or let her go forever. It was a standoff type of situation. She knew, I knew she knew. It was all we talked about. She just waited for me to come clean. I admitted it and asked if she still loved me, if we could try again. I told her I would never do anything to hurt her again. I made all the promises and pleaded. She finally said I could meet with her at her place. To her credit, she told me she was seeing someone by then, but that she would hear me out." Marlon stared out the window, afraid of his emotions as he spoke. It was like yesterday. He remembered how happy he was to be able to see her again. He had hope that he could fix things. He wanted so badly to start over.

He sipped his tea and was startled when the woman spoke up. A tiny voice from behind him.

"Did she take you back?" the woman inquired without shame.

Both Marlon and Andrea were startled. Marlon looked over at the woman and continued his story, in a slightly louder tone to include whatever busybodies might be listening.

"When I arrived at her place, she had the table set up. She baked an apple pie, my favourite, and had three cups on the table. I looked at her, then before I could ask, this big brother came into the kitchen. I am six foot three, so I am used to looking down on most guys. This guy was my height, but he was bigger, with broad shoulders and muscular. I was thinking, oh, okay. This is her man, and she wants to let me know what's up and tell me to stop bothering her. When she asked me to sit and cut me a slice of pie, I really didn't know what to say. He was one of them serious types, who doesn't talk a lot but when he does, you listen. He laid it out on the table. The man said he had been seeing Charlene and he thought she was the most amazing woman. I was sitting there thinking, I know she is amazing. No one needed to tell me this. Then he said something that blew my mind." Marlon set his empty cup on the tray table.

At this point the woman across the aisle was leaning towards Marlon, and the young girl behind his seat had turned around and listened from above Marlon's chair.

"His name was Anton...Anton Henry. He looked lika a middle-aged man, Fifty or so. Said he was married three times already and had come to terms with the failures of monogamy. 'The last thing I want in my later years is to own a woman.' He said that, own a woman. I remember thinking how many times I had said I wanted her to be mine. Yet here was this brother saying he didn't want to claim this prize as his own. He didn't want to be faithful and true to his woman. He didn't want to play by the rules of man, God, or anyone. I was sure at that moment I had won. What woman doesn't want a man of her own and to be his one and only? Even with my cheating past, I believed in that moment I was the victor. She was surely going to choose me, with our long history and this romantic comeback. I looked at him thinking, bro, you lost. He was so chill and relaxed; he wasn't even thinking of strategy. He knew what he was offering and was good with the outcome. I couldn't wait for my turn to speak, even though I felt it was already in the bag. I even wished at that moment I had brought a ring. There didn't seem to be any competition for me. This brother was big, good looking, athletic with long dreads. He was the thing women wanted, but he was straight out saying he was going to always be playing around in your face and that was that. I couldn't even breathe, I felt so confident. I tried to hold in my joy as I spoke. I cleared my throat and looked her in the eyes, her beautiful eyes, and I confessed my heart. I laid out a plan, I said I would be hers and hers only, forever and every day. I would make her feel and know she was what I wanted, needed and desired. When I finished, even the big man between us was crying. I thought that moment would be a good time for him to hang his head and take his big feet on out of there. But like a true competitor he stayed to hear her verdict."

Now the whole lower lever of the mega bus was listing to this man in the front row and the story he was relieving himself of.

"Charlene was almost blushing. She was trying hard not to burst into the happiness tears. She sipped her tea and looked at us both. Then she said:

'Marlon,' she said my name and I was just wishing I had a ring of some sort, something to seal this deal. Then I heard her say, 'For six months I waited for you to tell me the truth. I waited for you to tell me how a man can say he loves me for so long, then can cheat on me the first moment we come together. For six months I waited for you to explain this to me. In the six months as I waited, this beautiful man walks into my life. He has supported and been there for me in ways I never knew a man could. He told me not to give up on you, 'cause he knows you love me. But this love, this one love that closes the door on everything, is not what I am looking for anymore. I don't want one man forever, or marriage, I just want love that doesn't hurt. I am saying no to your relationship and yes to continue loving you. Because Anton doesn't need monogamy, so I choose this free life.'"

The women, including Andrea, were shocked. Eyebrows were racing upwards, some lips even settled as the audience thought about the situation.

"She chose him," the Trini lady said, "humph!"

"She chose her," Andrea said.

Marlon nodded. He could feel the weight of it. The choices, the decisions, the pain.

"I left Montreal heartbroken and deserved as much, which made it worse," he claimed.

"Did you…were you ever together again?" The woman asked.

Marlon smiled.

"Yes, once I understood what it all meant," he smiled.

"That didn't happen as quick as you might think…nope," he shook his head.

"Her being this free-loving woman meant I could still be there, and I still had a pawn in the game. You would think I would also get a happily ever after, but nope. I spent the first few years saying I could not get with that, my manhood, my religion, my worth would not allow it. So many more years were wasted because in the end…"

Marlon left the words dangling. Andrea and the other passengers left him to his thoughts and regrets.

Andrea knew his pain. She watched her mother's anger towards her father eat up her whole life. Her mother refused to even try again. She had been hurt too much. She knew what Marlon was living, he never got to love the woman the way he knew how to love and now he had run out of time.

Boston

Leesa was off after a ten-hour shift at the hospital. She flung her body into her favourite chair, too tired to even take off her jacket. An hour later she emerged from a hot bath with a bit more energy. On her fireplace mantle she placed the photo of Lena Horne, and beside it a small shooter glass with the word "My" in swirly glittering letters. She filled the glass with a shot of brandy and drank it down. "To Charlene, Lena and Michael." With a quick Facebook search, she found the page of Charlene Reese and read her many condolences. The old man was right. She was a beautiful woman, much like the clipping of the film star. She clicked on a few names and soon found herself on Anton Henry's page. His profile picture was of Charlene and him at a stop light on their bikes. It looked like an Advertisement from an Ebony magazine. They looked so in love, a picture of the perfect marriage. She felt sad for his loss. There were songs and poetry being post in her memory. Leesa decided to write a message to Anton to let him know about the passing of Michael. After all, Lena had meant so much to him. She also mentioned the shot glass, took a picture of it with her phone and attached it before sending the message.

Chapter 9

The night before the memorial, Shelly finally went home with her husband, Vern. She had been exhausted with all the phone calls, arrangements and small tasks. Thanks to Charlene, Shelly rarely thought about the death of her own mother. She died when Shelly was 20, before they ever had a chance to have an adult relationship. Now, both her actual mother and her motherly mentor were both gone. It was going to be hard. She was used to texting Charlene daily. She always checked in, even if either of them was traveling. Now everything was quiet. Vern knew she was feeling distraught, but also knew she was close to tears and didn't want her to break down, so he gave her space. "I just need to get through these next few days," she had convinced herself. She knew that her new life would consist of checking in on Pierre and Anton for the next few months.

*　　*　　*

Shirley and Dory were enjoying their trip After landing at the Montreal airport. Shirley booked an Uber to their downtown hotel. Both women fell in love with the French-Canadian city. The African driver said beautiful words to them as they exited his car. The air was chilly, but the city was breath-taking. After dropping their bags off inside, they headed out to shop. Shirley wanted to get a dress for the memorial. She had received an email from Ms. Valentine saying black clothing is not necessary, as Charlene was about colour and vibrant living. Shirley agreed with the message. "Colour, I can do!" she said to herself. The ladies went out into the cool November evening after learning where the best shopping area was located. Montreal was proving to be one of the greatest shopping places she had ever been to. Shirley feared she was easily going to put herself into debt from this trip. Dory was no help as she watched her friend heading towards the cash register with an armload of clothes.

*　　*　　*

Kevin separated from his grandfather shortly after they arrived in the city. It seemed they both needed a bit of space and alone time following the long drive. Kevin had Googled the area and searched out entertainment options. Putting on many layers of clothes, he headed out.

"I will be back in time to go to the service tomorrow," he promised before heading out of their lodging. Ash was content to just grab a beer and relax for the evening. He was less impressed when most of the television channels were only in French. He was okay to just sit back and replay his fond memories with Charlene.

*　　*　　*

Anton retired to his bed early. The next day would be a big day. He knew his emotions would be all over the place. There would be so many people, So many speeches. It would be the longest day of his life.

The condo was very quiet. A small bit of snow had fallen, leaving the streets in a white silence. Sara made two mugs of tea and crept quietly into the bedroom. Placing them on the night table, she climbed into bed beside Darrin.

"You keeping those pyjamas on?" she teased Darrin. He never once wore anything to bed back in the Netherlands. He had brought up all his belongings from the storage. Most of it was warm clothing, some papers, a pair of his rollerblades and his favourite plush pyjamas. "It's cold," he whined.

"At least they are not superheroes," Sara laughed.

"At least they are mine," he joked.

"You're so bad," she giggled.

"I thought Pierre took all his things," said Darrin.

"Nope, these are Anton's. I found a pair of slippers under the bed." She had not been looking, but when she had dropped an earring earlier, she found men's slippers. The first thing she noticed about Anton was his huge shoe size, so her detective skills confirmed the owner. They both laid quietly with their thoughts for a moment.

Sara laid back with the covers up to her face. She turned and looked at Darrin, not sure she even wanted to start the conversation. But also, not sure she could hold it in.

"How many are there?" she asked.

Darrin almost choked on his hot beverage.

"How many what?" He hoped he wasn't being asked about his mother's love life.

"Lovers, how many did she have?" Sara forged on.

Darrin turned towards her.

"I don't know, it's not exactly appropriate parent-child conversation. She...I don't know, okay. When I was young, the whole time she was raising me in the dance studio, as far as my memories serve me, she never had a man. She had no boyfriends and if she did, they didn't last long. To me, my mom had sex once, gave birth to me, and continued her life," he laughed. "I think all children think that," he concluded.

Sara laid back in the bed. There was still the one question she wanted answered.

"I guess you don't know about Pierre leaving her?" she asked.

Darrin sat up and smiled.

"As a matter of fact, that is the one story I do know. Mom emailed me photos from her last leg of the Canadian bike trip. There was a pic of her and Pierre, and she said he showed up in Ontario. She had been very surprised because they had broken up a year earlier and not talked since. She said it was hard on her because she really cared about him and he left her to start a family, or something like that. So, she was finishing her trip, about three days from reaching Montreal. She said she was setting up her tent at a camp site and he just showed up."

"How did he know?" She questioned.

"Well a lot of people knew. Many followed her on social media, and some even Googled her locations. She said she felt safer with many eyes on her. The year before, she had ridden three hours in the wrong direction. After that, she liked people being there to assist if needed," Darrin explained.

"After a year, he just showed up?" Sara was now completely invested in this drama of her boyfriend's mother.

"So, I know about Pierre, who else is there?" She desperately needed the salacious details. Charlene's love life and the stories around it had taken over Sara's thoughts.

"I really don't know," he laughed, 'I guess we will find out tomorrow."

"You don't think it's weird that you might meet like 20 men who were your mother's lovers tomorrow?" she asked intensely.

"I think 20 is a lot," he said, half teasing.

"You do know my mom did more in life than..." Darrin couldn't bring himself to finish that thought.

Sara nodded "I know, it's just so...not normal. I think about my mother, she only knew my dad, her whole life," Sara said. "I am not coming from a religious mind set, you know me, but I still have values and I just have hard time with this concept," she admitted.

"Well one man your whole life is also a concept that is strange to some. And remember my mother was not one to try to live under the same social rules as others do. During my early days, mom was like everyone else, hoping to find and marry that perfect guy. Then she moved to Montreal."

"And met Anton," Sara interjected.

"Met Marlon," Darrin corrected.

"Marlon?" Sara sat up in the bed. Marlon was a new player and Sara wanted the details on his story.

This Marlon character was the changing moment in Charlene's life. Sara couldn't be more interested.

"I remember she was in love. She wanted to marry him, she told me in secret. She had just moved here to Montreal and reunited with a guy from her past. He lived in Toronto. Anyhow, while I was visiting, he was staying with her. He was performing at some club. He was a singer. Pretty well known, I think. It was New Years. Anyhow, he left to go perform. I watched TV with her that night, but I was really watching her. She was quietly frantic. She knew he wasn't coming back. She didn't have a good track record with men up to this point, but somehow my mom just knew... she knew he wasn't coming back that night. She checked the clock so often. All night I could feel her energy. She was watching the door, the time, checking her phone. But like all the others he just disappeared. I don't really know why. My mom was beautiful and not an angry type. She was fun and easy going. But so many times, she thought a man would marry her...save her. And many times, she was disappointed."

"He never came back?" Sara waited for Darrin to continue.

He slowly shook his head "She waited up all night. She brought in the new year heartbroken. She tried to play it off, but I could tell. I had seen this so many times with her when I was growing up. Shortly afterwards, I returned to my travels and mom met Anton. I didn't see her again for about almost two years. I returned to Montreal and met my mom's new boyfriend. I got a quick introduction to her new lifestyle. She was now living a word I never even heard of at the time. I didn't fully understand it, but I liked Anton and they seemed happier than any other couple. She finally seemed happy. For a long time, I was mad at Marlon. I used to believe he broke my mother, but...now I see he was just the person who helped point her in the direction that was right for her."

"Were you upset or confused by her choice to be non-monogamous? Were you worried?" Sara asked.

'No, I was just glad my mom was happy. She finally seemed to have the love she was always looking for. And to be honest, it suits her. She was always in need of freedom and being able to just jet, so it really did seem like the right choice for her. It was just so unheard of at the time. I knew of no other person who had a relationship like Anton and my mom. But I also couldn't dispute the real love they seemed to have for each other. If you could have seen them together..." he mused.

"And the others?" she pressed.

"I don't know. Hmm, there was the American, Derrick...something. He worked offshore on an oil rig or something. And then there was another guy who sent my mom clothes." Darrin chuckled. "I don't know who my mom was involved with. Like I said, I am her child. We didn't talk about her sex or love life." Darrin balanced a spoon on his finger then twirled it around a few times.

Sara reached over to turn the lamp off.

"It's just a lot to understand," Sara said, as she switched off the lamp.

"So, this room…was it like their sex den?" Sara began.

"Shut up," Darrin tossed his pillow at her.

Ontario

Years Before

Charlene was waiting in line to pay for her camp site. A middle-aged woman stood in front of her, also waiting for the one teen on staff to explain the rules of the sites to the first customer in line. Charlene unbuckled her helmet and returned the smile the lady gave her.

"Bike camping?" she asked.

Charlene nodded. She was used to all the questions and people's thoughts on her adventures.

"Where are you coming from?" she asked.

It was the 900th time she had been asked that on this trip.

"Vancouver" She answered

The woman just stared at her like she had to have misheard.

"Did you say Vancouver?" she asked, her face looking like a question mark.

Charlene nodded.

"So, you are in a vehicle and then you ride?"

A small laugh came from Charlene.

"I rode my bike here from Vancouver," She clarified.

"Oh. Wow, that is incredible, by yourself? How much further are you going?" The woman didn't wait for answers. more questions kept coming.

"I am riding from here to Montreal," Charlene said patiently.

"Oh well I guess you're almost done! When did you start? How long ago? Sorry…" she offered a small laugh.

Charlene smiled. This was her every day, every stop conversation.

"Been on the road for over month now. Will be home day after tomorrow." Having not showered for days, Charlene was not comfortable standing and talking to people. She pointed to the counter at the front of the line, where the woman was now being offered service.

After her transaction, the woman wished her safe travels along with some religious affirmation, which Charlene just politely smiled at. After paying for her spot, Charlene jumped back on her bike to find the piece of grass she had paid for.

I hate paying to camp, *she thought. For most of the trip, she had just set up her tent in hidden bushes. But she had been too many days without a shower and people. Charlene found the matching number from her ticket on a post near a clearing. She had a fire pit, a picnic table and a tree. She hoisted her bike up against the tree and unpacked her bags. This had been her routine for the past month. Soon she would be back in her cosy condo with Anton. It would be fall soon, and she could get all her favourite paints at the craft stores before settling in for months of winter painting.*

The tent went up in minutes. She grabbed her toiletries bag and made her way to the showers. It always felt good to get a hot shower when she was bike touring. Some of her cleanings were quick cowboy style baths in the bathrooms of Tim Horton's, or a dip in the Saint Lawrence when she could. The steamy hot water felt so good to her pain ridden body. She didn't want to get out. She had picked up a full veggie footlong from Subway, which she was looking forward to devouring as soon as she got back to her site.

The night was just casting its first layer of darkness when she exited the showers. As she walked slowly back to her tent, many were starting campfires. Kids were still running around and using up their last bits of energy. She would just eat and jump into her sleeping bag and fall into a physical coma after supper. There was a figure standing at her site when she arrived. From a distance she thought it looked like Pierre, but laughed at the thought. She had not seen Pierre in over a year. When she reached her space, she gasped out loud. It was none other than Pierre LaVie, standing there before her. He was just as handsome as she remembered.

"I thought this was where you were, I checked online. You posted earlier this was your night target, the.. Glengarry campsite," he said.

Charlene was lost in a daze, unsure if this was real. She stood there with wet braids steaming in the cool night air.

Pierre moved towards her and kissed her on her cheek before she could snap out of her stupor.

Charlene moved past him, tossing her things into her tent and grabbing her food. He walked to the picnic table with her.

"I don't understand," she said, after eating the first bite. She had been excited about the Subway veggie sub in her backpack for the last two hours. Now she could hardly taste it.

"You have been following, I didn't know you even knew how!" She wasn't being malicious. She just knew Pierre was not computer savvy.

She is cute with her hair all braided like a girl, he thought to himself as he slid onto the bench beside her. She ate like she hadn't in days. He could only imagine what calories she burned on her rides. But she looked healthy and strong, tanned and beautiful.

Pierre wasn't sure what to say, even though he had practised the whole drive there.

"I made a mistake," he started. Charlene continued to eat as she silently pleaded for her love to return. Her feelings had all been packed away, but slowly began surfacing as she looked into Pierre's eyes.

Montreal

Kevin found himself in the heart of Montreal's night life. The street of Saint Laurent was riddled with night clubs, restaurants and late-night galleries. He wanted to walk around and check out the whole street, but the bitter cold forced him into one of the first bars he saw without a line up.

The bar was called La Belmont. It was packed with hot girls his age. He had read that Montreal had many Colleges in the city. Kevin passed through the relaxed door entry, checked his large winter coat and found a stool at the end of the bar. He watched as girls of all sizes and complexations roamed around him. Some brothers were dancing, but he never fancied himself as much of a dancer. He was content to drink his first Canadian beer and watch the ladies.

She approached him. A fine-looking dark-toned beauty with endless braids cascading down her backside. She said many words in French that were met by a dumbfounded look. As Kevin was thinking of how he could convey he didn't speak her language, he started using his hands to help. Waving them largely in front of her and speaking loudly, he said, "No Parle the French, I'm sorry, I'm American." A few people at the bar laughed at the big Black American.

Keena also chuckled as she slid onto a bar seat beside him.

"Most people just start speaking in English and everything is good," she said, with every hint of a French accent.

"Oh, you speak English, good," he smiled. She was pretty. A girl with her looks would never have sat down beside him like that in the States.

"Almost everyone does, it's Montreal," she laughed in a friendly way. "My name is Keena."

Kevin nodded, not trusting his words anymore. She was so beautiful. He didn't want to scare her away. Kevin introduced himself back and asked if she would like a drink. At least that was universal.

"You're visiting Montreal?" she asked.

"Yes, just arrived in the city about an hour ago," he smiled. "It was the longest drive of my life!"

"Where from?" she asked.

"North Carolina, that's my home, but I go to college in Georgia."

"Oh wow, you leave them warm southern places to come here in the middle of winter?" Keena gave him a crazy look.

"Now, I did not choose this trip, nope. This was my granddad's tour, he dragged me all the way across borders, get this, not even to visit someone or see something huge in he the history of the world. Nope, he dragged me all the way out here to attend a funeral. Some old girlfriend from his past died, and here we are. In Canada."

Keena looked at Kevin for a long time.

"A funeral…is it tomorrow?" she inquired.

Kevin nodded his head while signalling the bartender to bring two more drinks. "Yeah," he answered.

"Wait, are you going to Charlene Reese's celebration of life tomorrow?" she asked.

"You know her? She would be like 70 or something," he informed.

Keena laughed. "She was like 65. Yeah, I knew her. She was very well known in the Poly circles. She spoke at universities and was head of Montreal Black and Poly. Everybody knew Charlene," she explained.

"There is an organization?" he asked, blown away by the whole conversation. It seemed unbelievable to meet someone who knew the very reason he was there.

"Oui many, Montreal is a very progressive city. We have organizations and groups for everything," she confirmed. "I will be at the memorial service tomorrow too, but not the more personal one in the morning. That is special invite only. I will come after 1 o'clock. But I can watch some of that online," she stated.

"Online? Wow. So, she was really popular?" Kevin was now even more interested.

"Yeah but not in an international, Instagram way. She did a lot of things and was in a lot of circles, so she was known. But in the Poly world, she was like..."

"Yoda?" Kevin offered.

Keena burst into laughter. "Not Yoda, but yes, like a spiritual leader type. She didn't become open in her life until she was like 45 or 50 so to us, she seemed wise and all knowing. I went to one of her talks once, she was telling the people how love is not the rationed gift we use it as. She said that it is an endless supply which grows the more you give. This I remember, I hold this information very...umm I make it sacred information, you understand?" Keena tried to explain.

"She was like a mentor and counsellor for people who have relationship issues. And her husband, umm, Anthony, no Anton, yeah. They are this really cool older couple. He would hold meetings for the men and have talks too. I hope he continues to be a voice in the community. She was always living her best life. So, your granddad was one of her lovers?" she asked quite casually.

Kevin wasn't sure of his feelings at this moment. Was he proud that his grandfather had been connected to this all-loving, free-spirited woman? Was he embarrassed? Was he so smitten with Keena that he couldn't concentrate? Was the Canadian beer hitting him harder than he imagined? He felt completely overwhelmed.

"Uhh," unsure of words and translation, he just moved in and kissed her.

Keena laughed again.

"let's go," she said, detaching herself from the bar stool.

"Where?" Kevin asked.

"Chez moi," she smiled.

That, he understood. Montreal really is more progressive minded, he thought. Kevin texted his grandfather when he arrived at Keena's. A studio apartment only a few blocks from the bar.

"I will meet you at the service, I have the info. 10 a.m. Good night granddad."

Toronto

5:00 a.m

Aaron's son Fin took Cora and Aaron to the Toronto airport. The two were bickering in the car for the whole ride. Fin really wanted to go with them, to say goodbye to his cousin Charlene, but his wife had been sick and leaving her was not an option. He was granted permission to accompany the senior siblings all the way to the boarding gate until they were settled on the plane. He contacted his cousin Darrin and was assured they would be picked up as soon as they landed in Montreal. The airline hostess assured Fin she would keep an eye on Aaron and Cora during the flight.

Cora travelled light, with just an overnight bag. Her dress had been wrapped and folded in her bag along with her makeup and pills. Aaron wore his suit on the plane. He had no luggage with him.

"We will be back on the plane tomorrow," he said, quite content to wear his suit for the next 24 hours. Cora didn't have the energy to tell him he was being ridiculous.

Montreal

On the morning of the memorial, everyone had their work to do. Shelly had paid four teenaged girls from her building to help post pictures from Charlene's life all over the venue. One girl screamed when she saw how many boxes of photos existed.

"Wow, I never knew anyone to have this many pictures," she exploded cheerfully. The others grabbed boxes as they all found a section of the hall to start posting the life of Charlene Reese.

Darrin and Sara both went to the airport to receive his grandmother and his great uncle Aaron. Cora Reese was arriving at 7:45 a.m. Sara had rested at the airport Tim Horton's with two maple glazed donuts while Darrin went once more to check the board of arrivals.

"It's just landed, she should be coming down in about 15 minutes," he informed his girlfriend, who seemed more invested in her sticky treat. He was surprised at how much Sara liked the sweet pastries here. Back home she almost never gave in to sweets.

*   *   *

Tennessee James Parker came through customs at the other end of the Montreal airport. He had a small carry-on bag with him and exited the terminal into the cold, windy air. A taxi quickly loaded him and brought him to his lodging in the central part of Montreal. He had time to lay his suit out, take a hot shower, shave and dress. He retrieved a small paper bag out of his luggage and placed it next to the door. "Don't want to forget that," he said to himself before spraying his cologne on his chest. Montreal was a new kind of cold. He had only brought his long formal coat and he knew that was not going to keep his southern body warm. He walked as fast as he could, with intention and sparkling frost under his boots, to the location typed into his GPS. It was a hall of some sort. A few folks were outside waiting and smoking. He slid his thin frame through the doorway and entered the life of Charlene.

*   *   *

Cora was over the moon when she saw her grandson coming towards her. He looked so much like her baby girl. She had not seen Darrin in some years. The eighty-nine-year-old woman looked stunning in her shoulder-length, all-grey hair style with dyed purple tresses on the ends of one side.

"Always the stylish one," Darrin greeted his grandmother.

"look at you," she smiled.

Darrin's uncle Aaron reached in for a hug after Cora. "You look good," he said with a huge grin. Sara stood in the background of their reunion until Darrin pulled her in for introductions.

"Nana, this is my girlfriend Sara, and this is my nan's brother uncle Aaron," he waved his hands around as he introduced them. Sara's instinct was to reach in with a handshake, but by now she knew all Darrin's people were huggers. So, they hugged.

"I am going take you to the hotel to get dressed and then we will go straight to the venue, okay?" Darrin instructed.

"I am all ready," his uncle declared.

"What about Anton?" Cora asked, ignoring her brother.

"We have to meet him there, he had lots to do this morning," Darrin stated.

Cora nodded. She always liked Anton. He was a calm spirit. Cora hoped to lean on his solidness a bit throughout this day.

Chapter 10

S helly's husband Vern had been put in charge of dealing with the caterers. They were soon busy unloading and preparing the food. Tea, coffee and pastries were being placed on a long table. Vern gave orders for the food to be refilled on the hour. He hired one of his friends to serve hot cider and mulled wine. The day was quite cold. Many of the out-of-town guest were not prepared for the shock of Montreal winter.

Shelly knew there would be no time to go home and change, so she found herself in the bathroom of the hall getting dressed and doing her makeup. She had about ten minutes before people would start arriving. She had received a text from Darrin saying he was 15 minutes away. Anton and Pierre had also texted their estimated time of arrival. The hall looked beautiful, a mixture of class and sophistication with a dash of wild and zany to reflect Charlene in her many ways. Waves of feelings begged for Shelly's attention. She tried to keep her own emotions in check as so many around her were cracking.

Charlene's cycling partner Yves Pinot had volunteered to have many of Charlene's paintings placed around the room. He could be heard barking French orders to the men who carried the precious pieces into the space. When Yves saw Charlene's bike being wheeled in, he almost fell. Shelly quickly made her way over and lead Yves to a chair. The frail man just pointed to the bike and cried," Oh mon dieu!"

People started pouring in a few minutes before the start time. Noise levels rose as people made their way through the hall of a thousand photos and into the large receiving room. Shelly then realized how big this was going to be. They decided to hold the life celebration all day, so as not to overload the venue. Caterers were to bring in food on the hour until 9 p.m. Musical friends of Charlene were coming and would play throughout the day. An online video stream had been set up to broadcast for those who could not attend. Shelly was exhausted by the time the doors opened. Vern gave her a warm hug and whispered his love in her ear. She was happy she had filled her purse with packages of tissue. Taking a deep breath, Shelly made her way to the end of the photo hall to receive the guests.

Cora arrived first, escorted by her grandson, Sara and her brother Aaron. Cora was breathtaking. She was wearing a red dress with a silk scarf around her flowing grey hair. Even in her most senior years, Cora made people stop and look. Darrin was worried about his grandmother. She now had laid all her children to rest. She was so much smaller in appearance. She seemed to be more confused. Granted, she was almost 90 years old. Earlier in the morning, he had seen his nanny have a breakdown. "All my girls are gone," she had cried. Darrin spent the morning trying to lift his nan's spirits. She needed a moment, but once she put that red dress on, she wiped her face, put on her lipstick and announced she was ready.

They looked around them at the hall of memories. Cora was wonderfully surprised at the sheer volume of photos posted along the entrance. That was one thing Charlene and Cora had in common, they both loved taking and being in photos. Darrin, not so much.

"Do I have time to look at this?" She asked Darrin, sounding childlike.

"Yes, lots of time,' he answered.

Uncle Aaron appeared to be less excited about standing for that long of a time.

"I am going in, I need to sit down," he mumbled.

"You just do that," she spat back.

Cora took Sara's arm, making it known she was to stay and walk Cora through the maze of photos.

Darrin smiled at his lady before rushing off into the hall.

"Oh look, that is from when we went to Mexico! And look, this is a baby picture. I had that taken when she was three. Oh, the first picture of

Darrin and Charlene. Oh, these are all my girls..." The photo walls made Cora especially happy as she slowly made her way through.

Shirley and Dory stepped into the hall next, and gasped at the unbelievable amount of Charlene's images posted on every surface of wall space.

"Oh wow," said Shirley. Both women moved slowly while viewing the montage of Charlene's life.

"She really lived a full life, didn't she?" Dory whispered to her friend. Shirley nodded. There was an elderly lady in a stunning red dress being guided by a young white woman ahead of them. Shirley moved herself and Dory to the other side, so as not to disturb the woman in her very real memory lane session.

"This is her husband and her," Shirley pointed to a photo of Charlene and Anton. "Oh, and here he is, this is Pierre," The photo of Charlene and Pierre was up high, and Shirley stood on her toes to point it out.

"They are both very handsome men. I am liking Miss Charlene's taste," Dory whispered and the two giggled as they continued down the aisle.

Anton stood alone in the large room. All the chairs had been set up, the stage was beautifully decorated, six paintings were strategically placed around the room and Charley's bike was on display in front of the stage. Everything looked perfect. He looked at Shelly and hugged her with a smile as she scurried around finishing last minute details.

Darrin made his way over to Anton. They both seemed pleased with their surroundings.

Three musicians set up and began to play some bossa nova. The music made the mood light and relaxed. Shelly had repositioned herself at the front of the room to welcome the gathering people. Anton and Darrin joined her.

James entered the hall dressed in cowboy boots and an all-white suit. He had gold rimmed glasses on and a shiny bald head. Anton recognized him immediately. Darrin and Anton approached the flashy American.

"Darrin," Tennessee James smiled.

"You must be Anton," the men did a hand-shake-turned-hug.

"It's been a long time," James looked back at Darrin.

Darrin membered the man from a very long time ago. He marvelled at the length of time his mother kept people in her life.

"You came all the way from Memphis?" Darrin asked.

'I sure did, I would have come from the North Pole to say goodbye to that lady," James patted Darrin on the back.

"This here is really something. Charlene loved her some pictures." James slowly did a full circle turn taking in all the magnificence of the photo tribute. Darrin chatted a bit before being pulled into many directions for introductions and hugs.

Darrin had been busy greeting people. Sara wandered around the hall trying to blend into the colourful crowd. She couldn't believe the blunted disrespect for death. She could understand not wearing black, but these people were practically in costume. Sara watched two Black women dressed in animal prints as they inched along the walls of photos, making noises and gestures, pointing to random pictures. *This is more like a circus than a funeral*, she thought. *This would never happen in my family.*

Ash and his grandson Kevin entered the building quietly. Kevin had already walked straight through the hall before noticing that his granddad had stopped at the entrance and was slowly taking in all the photos. Not wanting to disturb his grandfather, Kevin found a plate and a drink and made himself comfortable in the back row of the seating. The place was huge, and all the pictures made it feel warm and cosy. Kevin had made plans to meet Keena there later in the day.

Shirley stood dead in her spot, excited with her find in the massive photo show. She had found one photo of her, Charlene and Derrick. She pointed it out to Dory. "Look" she pointed.

"I took that," a French accent spoke from behind them.

Shirley was shocked and elated to see Pierre standing there. They hugged and she introduced her friend Dory. Dory smiled in agreement, remembering Shirley's description of this man. He looked older and greyer than the old photo Shirley was still pointing to.

"I am so happy to see you. I am so sorry for your loss. Were you two still close?" Shirley asked.

Pierre nodded. "She was...we...yes," Pierre had tears in his eyes and Shirley just hugged him again, not sure what else to do. They stood in the middle of the photo gallery just holding each other.

Marlon waited on the front steps of the building. He had received a text from Andrea saying she would be there at exactly 10:45. The Montreal air was chilly, and he really should have brought a heavier coat. Marlon held the door when he saw an elderly woman trying to push her way out.

"Mrs. Reese!" he said, happy to see her. The woman he thought should have been his mother in law looked to be making an escape. Cora Reese recognized the singer immediately. Charlene used to jump on a bus to Toronto for Marlon's concerts, and had invited her to see Marlon perform a few times. She and Charlene would get a hotel room in the city and get all dressed up. He had aged, Cora thought. She knew Charlene and Marlon had been in love for as long as she could remember. Charlene was secretive about why things didn't work out, but Cora could tell the moment they saw each other that they were in love. She might never understand how Charlene could love so many, but she was sure of two things: Anton Henry was Charlene's soul mate, and Marlon Styles was her great love. But who wasn't, she thought, as she briefly reflected on Charlene and her over-inflated love life?

"Marlon, is that you? My God, we are all so old," she smiled.

"Speak for everyone but yourself Ms Cora, because you still look like a fox," Marlon hugged the woman gently. She was smaller than he ever remembered. Her grey hair was poised like she had just left the salon.

"Where are you off to? It's cold out here," he asked, concerned.

"I was looking for my grandson, Darrin, I didn't see him inside." Her voice was small and she looked frail. He knew Cora and Charlene often clashed. Cora would never understand Charlene's need for freedom, or why she so adamantly refused marriage and the natural courses of life. Charlene often battled with her mother on visits to Toronto and would complain constantly to Marlon with her old-school mother issues. But looking at Cora now, Marlon couldn't help but feel great pain for Cora's loss.

"Let's try to find him together," he said convincingly as they re-entered the hall.

Fixing his gaze straight ahead, Marlon didn't let his eyes steer to either side, where thousands of photos of his love were posted from floor to ceiling. He stepped slowly and steadily alongside the frail woman as they entered the large room ahead.

The room was beautiful with flowers and Charlene's art. Tables were along the back with food and hundreds of chairs set up. Some folk had already claimed their seats. He saw Anton ahead speaking with a short lady he thought at first to be a child. Then he saw Darrin come rushing towards them.

"Nana, I was looking for you. I need you to stay in your seat, we are starting soon." Darrin's tone held stress and concern. He was about to reach for his grandmother's arm when he recognized the man assisting her. It was Marlon Styles, the singer. The very last man to break his mother's heart. His memory flashed back to the big Jamaican man with the soft voice. Marlon Styles was the very man his mother waited up for, the man who never showed. Darrin tried to adjust his face to the friendly host he had been working on. but Marlon saw it. He saw the look of contempt flash through Charlene's very face. It was awkward and painful. Marlon released Cora to the protection of Darrin and went to find his seat.

"Do you know him?" Cora asked when Marlon was out of ear shot

Darrin nodded. He had not expected to see Marlon ever again.

Marlon searched for Andrea once more before finding his seat. He was informed his name was on one of the roped-off seats.

Three seats were lined up close to the stage. Darrin sat in one, his regal-looking grandmother sat in another, and the third chair was empty. The black velvet curtain was closed. People were asked to take their seats. On the left were five rows of seats sectioned off with names on them. On the right, others clamoured to find a seat.

Sara watched as the seats filled up on the left. Men of all ages and backgrounds plucked their name tags off the chairs and greeted the others next to them. Sara was seated near the front of the right-hand side, next to Charlene's best friend Tonya from her childhood.

"You are Darrin's girlfriend?" A woman asked, making friendly conversation. Sara nodded.

"I am Keena, I knew Charlene from the Poly groups, and my boyfriend's grandfather was one of her lovers," She smiled.

Sara nodded and kept her eyes on Darrin. He was seated, holding his nan's hand.

Chapter 11

The Service

Anton and Shelly stepped onto the stage. Anton looked so stately in his African garb. Shelly was in a pale pink dress and heels that lifted her merely to the height of Anton's chest. He was slouched, trying not to overshadow his petite friend next to him. They looked like a stand-up comedy team. Shelly held Anton's hand as she promised she would during his speech to Charlene's people.

"Welcome," Anton said softly. His voice went unheard. Anton and Shelly both saw the tech guy making many hand gestures. Anton quickly adjusted the wireless mic clipped onto his collar. He stepped up and tried again.

"Good morning," his voice boomed through the hall. Cora sat up in her seat and gave her son-in-law her attention. Many scattered to find a seat. Anton looked down at the front row. It was filled with Charlene's most special loved ones. Many men of many ages, shapes and cultures occupied those chairs. All people who shared the many stories that made up Charlene's life. Her cycling partner, her art curator, her best friends and lovers.

"Good morning everyone! My name is Anton Henry, for those who do not know me. I am Charlene Reese's...husband," he spoke slowly.

120

The room was respectfully silent. Shelly squeezed Anton's hand. She felt like a little girl holding her dad's big strong hand.

"This celebration of life is being broadcast through a streaming media source. The gentleman in the red is here to show the tributes coming in from across the world and, when you're ready to give a speech, he will mic you," Anton pointed to the tiny microphone on his collar.

"We are starting today's tribute with words from Charlene's most beloved, her son, Darrin," Anton and Shelly stepped back and took their chairs to the side of the stage, where Cora waited.

Darrin stood and moved to where Anton and Shelly had been. He hugged Shelly and nodded to Anton. Not having a mic to hold was bothersome to him. He needed a fiddling tool. Reaching in his pocket he found a coin. He flipped the quarter in his fingers as he spoke.

Darrin was wearing his favourite purple shirt with a blue tie. His mother would have loved to see this image of him. His hair was pushed back off his handsome face. Charlene never put parental pressures on her child. She knew how important freedom of expression was. She never fussed over his clothes, career choices or love interest. She let him make choices and stood behind his decisions.

When Darrin was a small child, he had big floppy curls. As much as she tried to comb them out and tie his hair neatly behind his head, he wouldn't permit it. "Too Mexican," he would claim, after seeing the men from the soccer commercials. Darrin never liked the attention or the fuss, he preferred simple.

Darrin looked out into a completely full room. There were people standing where the chairs ended. No one moved except the staff. People patiently and respectfully waited for him to commence. Darrin's eyes stopped at the reserved section. Five rows of chairs seated men over the age of 50. Some of his mother's best friends and some relatives. It was a bit overwhelming. Then, Sara's inquiries jumped into his thoughts. The long row of men...*they couldn't all be...*He shook the thought out of his head. He had had enough of the sex shaming conversations with his mother back in the day. There were just so many people. So many he knew, so many he had forgotten and so many he didn't know. His mother had lived so many lives. Even he could never know everything about Charlene.

"Good morning everyone, my name is Darrin Reese. Yes, I know many of you, but not everyone. My mother knew and loved so many people. It would be almost impossible to know you all," he smiled.

"My mother's life expanded to places and depths most of us could never get to. She has friended and befriended so many people worldwide. I travelled the world with my mother, I learned all my great skills from her." The crowd smiled and nodded knowingly.

"My mother was the kind of woman who cared about others and helped so many. She was quiet about that side of herself. She used to travel with kids toys in her bag and would just put a super ball in the hands of a child just to watch their face light up. Or once, we were in Marrakesh and she gave these boys packages of toy airplanes, just simple paper toys. She made strangers feel joy in her presence. She reached out to people and made time for them. Her biggest gift was spending time with people. She made time and reserved time to just be there. To listen, to teach and guide. My biggest problem in life when I was a child was sharing my mother. Everyone wanted to spend time with her. I remember being just a kid, and so many of the neighbourhood children would come over. She fed everyone with the little we had. She listened to young girls and their problems, she did so much for our community. Everyone knew and loved Charlene Reese, and I was so proud when people asked if I was Charley's boy. I used to be angry when others took her attention from me because she was my mom. I soon realized the same thing all of you would have to come to know, you can't own Charlene Reese. You can only be in the inner circles of her love. She loved. Charlene's biggest legacy is that she loved. And looking at the enormous amount of people here and the huge list of followers on the monitor, she loved and she was loved and she will be missed by the masses." Darrin stopped to allow his beautiful words to linger, but he found his feelings were coming on too strong. He looked over and saw Shelly waving a tissue. He quickly reached for it and cleared his throat to continue.

"You can tell from the millions of photos Shelly and her team have assembled throughout this space, that love was my mother's greatest gift." A rumble of sounds followed Darrin's words.

"Some of you followed my mother's great cycling adventures. She was fearless in the world. She packed her bike and left for weeks at a time, enjoying a world most of us have never seen before. Then she would come back and paint and pour her beauty into her colourful paintings. There are few lives as beautifully lived ad Charlene Reese's. If you have danced with her, toured or travelled with her, had a cup of tea and a story, or just been with her in her warmth, then you are a very fortunate person."

The crowd let go of a cheer for Darrin and his lovely speech. The next speech was in 20 minutes and would be given by Cora Reese. But everyone stayed in their seats as Marlon Styles stepped on to the platform.

He gave Anton a quick hug before cuing the band. The crowd settled down when the music started. The performer had come from the reserved seating. Many were making speculations. Others knew exactly who Marlon Styles was.

With a voice soft and smooth like Smokey Robinson, Marlon sang a beautiful rendition of Ray Charles's "Can't Say Goodbye". He sang with purpose and emotion. He left no one without tears. The song ended and somehow Marlon was unable to move. Andrea made her way through the crowd and onto the stage. She took Marlon's hand and guided him off and back to his seat. Marlon was in tears as he took his chair. The man next to him patted him on the back.

"That was beautiful, brotha," Ash said.

Marlon extended his hand and introduced himself. "Marlon Styles," he said.

"Ashford Adams, call me Ash," they shook hands and Marlon nodded.

"How long have…how far back do you and Char…?" Marlon was still fighting off tears and struggling to speak. But he tried to make conversation.

"I have known that lovely creature for just over 27 years. I worked it out on the drive up," Ash smiled and asked, "You?"

"Over 45 years," Marlon said. "I met her when she was 19 years old and fell in love with her on sight."

Ash nodded knowingly.

Just then, Cora Reese was assisted by her grandson to the stage. Many put down their drinks and snacks as they waited for Darrin to clip a mic on his grandmother. Her voice was tiny and Darrin gave the tech guy a gesture to pull the volume up for her.

"Can you all hear me," her tiny voice carried through the room. She received ample affirmation she was being heard. Cora didn't know what to do with the absence of a podium or a mic in her hand. She just stood there in front of so many people. Some she had met before, some she had forgotten, many she never knew. The string of handsome men in front of her made her blush.

"This is the third and last time I am speaking on behalf of one of my daughters. They are all gone now," Cora paused, hoping the words were going to push through her mouth.

"I never expected to outlive my most rebellious and defiant daughter. I was sure she would be on the earth long after I was gone. Lord have mercy, Charlene Reese was my youngest daughter. She was a creative child who danced all the time. She was either dancing or doing cartwheels as a child. She was always doing the things she wanted to do in life." Cora looked out into the audience again. She looked at Maron Styles, the man she knew loved her daughter, and the French man in the front row, she had recognised him from visits in the past. Cora's mind wondered about all the other men. Were they all lovers? They were many, all striking men for their age. She could feel the heat rise again in her face. She continued to speak even though she lost track of the speech she had rehearsed.

"She did do whatever she wanted, but the world is not ours to just do what we like. There are rules and consequences. I never could have everything..." she trailed off.

Anton's head popped up, followed by many others. Did Charlene's mother just start slagging off her dead daughter? Darrin was the fasted out of his seat. Cora's manor had changed.

"You can't just have everything." Her voice had gotten stranger as Darrin and Sara guided Cora off stage quickly, behind the curtain and down the long hallway.

"You calm her," Darrin instructed Sara and he rushed back onto the stage. His intentions were to make apologies and move on to the next speaker or music number.

"So sorry," Darrin jumped back onto the stage and tried to quiet the room. He had not realized he couldn't be heard until another voice had boomed through the room.

"I understand exactly what you are feeling. I thought I was the only person in this world who doesn't hail the queen of a thousand lovers. I have never been around so many people who act like this is normal as breath. Her disrespect for the way of love, God, and the natural path of matrimony leaves me entirely baffled. All these people acting like Charlene was the greatest woman known to mankind, when she just fucked her way through life. We could have done that you know..." Sara was releasing, and it came out without filter or shame.

It took half a second for Darrin to realize that it was his girlfriend Sara speaking, but much longer for him to find them. Darrin ran through the building trying to locate his nan and Sara. People in the seats acted as people do when drama is high. Shirley covered her mouth and looked to Dory, who tried ever so hard not to laugh.

In an attempt to help, Marlon joined Anton back on stage.

"I can do another song, until Cora and that gets settled," he whispered to Anton.

"That would be great," Anton cued the musicians to return to their instruments. Everyone smiled when the first bars of the song began.

"She's some kinda wonderful..." Pierre began, singing out loud.

James nodded. "Quite fitting," he agreed.

Darrin was beyond angry. He always knew of the ongoing rift between his disapproving grandmother and his mom, but to hear the woman he had hoped to marry saying the things she had just said made him livid. He moved swiftly, trying not to break into a jog. It took a few minutes to locate them, but the sounds from the crowd indicated the conversation was still ongoing. He found them at the end of a long corridor. The first thing he did upon finding them was grab his nan gently, pull her mic off and disarm it. This mere action revealed to Sara that she had been overheard by the masses of mourners.

Instant embarrassment and regret flashed across her flushed face.

"Darrin," she pleaded.

"Nan, can you please go back to your seat?" Darrin's voice was sharp. Sara had not seen this side of him before. His face looked exactly like Charlene's in the argument they last hashed out.

Cora had also just figured out that their conversation was not private. She was less ashamed than Sara.

"Darrin, sweetheart, don't be angry with this young lady. She was just relaying her concerns," his grandmother felt the need to defend Sara. On any other occasion, he would have thought that to be sweet. But this was just another time when his grandmother was looking for an ally against his mother, at her own funeral no less. Darrin was not letting this happen.

"Darrin I just," tears started to fill Sara's eyes. She could hardly catch her breath. She kept trying to remember every word she had just spoken and think of damage control at the same time.

"Just what?" he snapped. "Just flew thousands of miles to talk trash about my mother at her funeral?" Darrin was both yelling and whispering. His face was twisted into a look that scared Sara. In no culture is it okay to speak ill of a man's mother, and never at her funeral. She could feel the gravity of it all now.

Sara wanted to collapse. She was hurt and angry about what had just happened. She needed to explain herself, but her emotions broke and all she could muster were cries.

"Don't blame this young lady, she is all out of sorts with hormones," Cora re-entered the conversation.

"Nan this is not...wait, what about her hormones?"

Sara went bright red, her face burned from ear to ear. "I..."

"She's pregnant, isn't she?" Cora asked and told at the same time.

Sara stumbled, "I...how...I didn't...How did you know that?" She managed.

"'You ain't never met an old Black woman before have you?" Cora teased and left the two young ones to talk.

"It's true? You are?" Darrin demanded, hoping the anger in his voice had mellowed.

Sara nodded. This was so not the way she had envisioned telling him.

"I thought I would wait until we returned to Europe to tell you. I thought it was best to know what kind of relationship we are having first," She took deep breaths to allow herself to speak.

"Wait, what do you mean relationship? Are you thinking about leaving?" Darrin could feel the heat rising up from his collar. His emotions were all over the place.

"No, I am not leaving. It's you, and it's this," Sara pointed to the montage of photos.

"I can't be in this relationship and give birth to a baby knowing that you may decide sometime in your forties or fifties to leave and have many women. It all seems so normal here to these people, but believe me, it is not. I cannot continue this knowing what I know." Her voice stopped. She had come to a loss for English words. A whole slew of Dutch words followed. Darrin tried not to laugh, thinking about the old Ricky Ricardo clips he watched with his mom. When she stopped, both her and Darrin broke into a tension release of laughter.

"Darrin reached for Sara and held her tight."

"No, my love, no. I know how hard this must have been for you, everyone saying how much like my mother I am, but no. I am not like that. I still believe in one man and one woman. I want to be together with you and have a family, for all the forevers." She looked at him, trying to wipe away all the wet parts of her face.

"I am so sorry, I wanted to wait too, until we were back but..." Darrin reached in his pocket.

He had taken out a single item. There was no box, it wasn't wrapped in anything. It was a white gold band with a solitary diamond set in it.

"I had intended to ask in a much grander fashion, but what's more important is for you to know my intentions right now," he looked down to see if it was a safe and clean area to traditionally kneel.

Sara's face bloomed. She couldn't believe what had just happened. She grabbed Darrin and held him tight.

"Yes, yes! To marriage, babies and all the forevers."

Moments later, Darrin and Sara returned to the service. Pierre had just sung a French song and nodded to Anton as he moved off the stage. Anton made an announcement, inviting anyone up to speak. There was a sign-up list for order. Every hour someone would read from the online tributes. It was beautiful to see friends of Charlene's, loved ones, and the community all speak their love and admiration. Everyone had been so touched and moved. In between speakers, Anton made an announcement inviting anyone holding a special gift from Charlene to join him backstage.

There was a little commotion from the crowd as everyone settled in to hear the beautiful poetry from Darrin's childhood friend, Idris. Anton waited backstage holding a special bottle of prosecco. He remembered Charlene always preferred this to champaign when celebrating. There were so many tiny details and specialties that he would always remember about her.

He placed the bottle on a small round table. Next to it was a small shot glass with the word "love" hand-written in glitter. This was Anton's shot glass.

James was the first to pull the curtain back and join Anton. They shook hands as James placed his identical looking glass on the table. Anton leaned over to read the word.

"Heart," he smiled. He never knew who had received these little hand-painted trinkets his wife had made so many years ago.

"I can't. She gave me one, and I am honoured to be in this inner circle. I just don't believe I belong," James said.

"She must have loved you," Anton smiled. "which means, you belong."

"We…we didn't have a relationship like you or the French guy. I couldn't do this big love and be an open thing with her. We just hung out, then I got married and Reesy and I just played computer games. We weren't having, like, an affair or nothing like that," James said.

"Doesn't mean she didn't love you, just because you didn't join in on her lifestyle. She must have cared if she continued to do something like play a game with you daily, and I know it was daily. I watched her log on and play. It meant a lot to her to continue a friendship and stay connected to you, that was exactly one of the things she like most about being a polyamorous woman, she could continue relationships past their romantic time. She could love on all wave lengths."

James appreciated these words from Anton. He had heard a lot about the guy but was really glad to finally make his acquaintance. Ash walked in after, followed by Pierre. Pierre pulled his little glass from his jacket pocket. The word was written in French, "Sentir".

"To feel," he translated. Everyone nodded. Pierre's glass looked older. The glitter was almost worn off. It looked like he had already had a few drinks from it.

Ash's glass said, "You". He smiled as he lined his glass up with the others. Marlon was next to enter. He found a place in the circle of men and looked at the table. A hopeless look covered his face as he reached into his bag to place his contribution. His glass looked like none of the others. It was slightly taller and had the name of a city covered with masking tape. He had hand-written the word "Me".

"'I lost mine long time ago," he admitted. His voice soft and gentle.

"Is that all of them?" Ash asked.

Everyone looked to Anton as he threw his shoulders up, claiming no knowledge.

"I don't know how many there were," He admitted.

"I got one," a sweet voice said, entering from behind the felt curtain.

Shirley had made her way into the circle. She was all smiles as she knew she understood the email correctly. She had found Derrick's glass after his death and knew she had to come and take part in this beautiful tribute on his behalf.

"My late husband's," she said, to wipe the smirk off James's face.

"There was another, I got a call from a hospital in Boston. Michael Sylvia had a glass on him when he passed. His said, 'Life,'" Anton announced.

"Charley also had one," said Anton.

One more was added to the collection. Everyone looked up to see Darrin.

"Mom and I had the same one," he said.

Marlon turned it around. In perfect fancy glitter, it read, "forever".

They all smiled as Darrin popped the bottle and poured a little into each glass.

"Please don't drink until everyone has said their toast," Darrin instructed.

Anton spoke first as he held up his little glass of bubbles.

"My darling Charley, you will be missed by many. I am so grateful you choose to share a life with me and keep me in love and laugher all these years."

The others raised their glasses, and then lowered.

Pierre stepped up like a co-pilot, raised his glass and spoke in French.

"Vous mes beaux reves vous etes mon coeur, mon ame, chacun de mes reves. Tu me manques pour tourjours."

Anton understood the beautiful words and raised his glass as the others followed. Shirley couldn't keep the smile from her face. Pierre sounded like one of those French movie stars. She knew her thoughts were bordering on inappropriate, so she shook her head to clear her thoughts.

Ash stepped forward next, raising his little shot glass.

"My beloved Charlene, I enjoyed every moment we had together, and only wish there could be more. I have lived a life of driving fast cars, but nothing beats the adventure of being with you."

Again, glasses were raised to a small murmur of agreement. Marlon covered his eyes and waited, not sure if he could add his words. Tennessee James stepped up.

"My Reesy. You played the game of life and won every time, like a champion," James raised his glass.

Anton smiled, Ash nodded, and they all raised their glasses.

Darrin watched as the bubbles settled in his glass.

Shirley was next. She cleared her throat to speak up. She looked over at Pierre who was already staring into her brown eyes. Shirley felt a warmth.

"Charlene meant a lot to my husband. He introduced us, and I will never forget the night I met the most alive and amazing woman. I am so glad I had a chance to know Charlene Reese. Cheers to her beautiful presence, and to being here, holding this glass with her most beloved," Shirley toasted.

They lifted their glasses once again. With only Marlon and Darrin left, the two made eye contact. Marlon stepped forward.

"I have loved Charlene since we were just young, wide-eyed kids. She blew me away the first time and every time I saw her. I…" Marlon took a deep breath. The others waited patiently.

"I am truly lucky to have known this forgiving and loving woman, who gave me chances I didn't deserve. To Charlene."

After raising his glass, Darrin finished the toast.

"My mother was the sun many of us moved around. She will be missed, but remembered with smiles and warmth. She was a woman ahead of her time. She leaves a legacy of love behind her."

Darrin led the group as he brought his glass to his mouth and drained it.

He placed the empty glass on the table. He looked at everyone and then started to line the glasses up like a puzzle.

"What was the missing one?" he asked Anton

"My" Anton answered.

"Right," moving all the shot glass around, Darrin soon came to a perfect combination, leaving a space for the absent one.

Everyone read the words together.

"My…love…heart…feel…joy…you…me…forever."

Chapter 12

Kevin packed the car up and waited in the passenger seat for his granddad.

Ash moved slowly down the outside staircase, letting the cool winds attack his face. He had never felt this type of cold before. He felt alive and refreshed. The service made him feel better. He felt less like he lost someone and more like he gained a clear understanding of love and grief.

Ash climbed into the driver's seat and smiled at Kevin.

"You ready?"

Kevin nodded. He was about to select music from his phone, then decided not to.

"She was quite a lady," he said.

"Sure was," Ash drove slowly through the narrow streets. A light snow flurried around the car, not quite dusting the ground.

"I like it here," Kevin said. It's cold as hell. But I like it."

They drove a couple hours and quickly made it through customs into the states.

They talked about Kevin's classes, the long drive, Keena, Ash's lady friends and his race career.

"I wish I could have seen you race granddad. Me and Kenny watched some videos, but I wish I could have been there."

"Me too, I was fast. I was the first Black man to win an auto speedway first-place trophy," he bragged.

"When I got into the driver's seat and felt that steering wheel and smelled that diesel and heard that engine roaring…"

Ash stopped speaking and Kevin instantly noticed the car had picked up speed.

"Granddad, you're gonna get yourself a ticket," Kevin teased.

Ash looked over at him and smiled. The speedometer was moving steadily on the dash.

Kevin sat back in his seat, holding tight to the seat belt.

Ash exceeded eighty, then a hundred, and kept increasing.

The car had passed every vehicle in its path. Kevin held on to the dash. He was both scared and exhilarated. The sound of highway patrol was in the distance. Ash still kept his foot down. He made it to an exit before the two police cars caught up. Veering off the exit ramp, Ash reduced his speed as Kevin watched the two patrol cars zoom past.

Ash pulled into a gas stop where he and Kevin enjoyed a coffee and laugh.

"Just a little further to your uncle Buddy's. Let's take the scenic roads," Ash opened the door to the driver's side. Kevin tossed his empty cup into the garbage and got into the passenger's seat.

*   *   *

James arrived in Memphis at 7 p.m. sharp. In all his travels, he had never found anyone waiting at the airport for him before. He was touched to see Marcy standing in the receiving line. She was smiling and threw her arms around him. She was dressed nicely in a bright floral dress. He sure was glad to take off his coat. *If I never see a cold winter again, that's fine with me*, he thought.

"I am so glad you are back, and I missed you," She said.

James felt flushed. Marcy had never just spoken her feelings so easily. He was excited to get to know this new version of her.

'Let's go home," he whispered in her ear.

"Did you have a good time?" she asked.

James nodded.

"I learned a lot of things about a lot of things," he smiled. "Let's grab some take-out and I will tell you all about it."

Marcy took his free hand in hers and started walking.

*　　*　　*

Yves Pinet put on his winter ride gear and brought his heavy winter bike outside into the bitter cold day. He got on and rode through his neighbourhood. His face was covered and every bit of skin hidden from the elements. He came to a park and stood his bike up against a snow-covered tree. Taking out a cigarette, he lit it and puffed the smoke into the clear crisp air. The tears were iced into the thin cracks of his face. Yves looked at the solo track his bike made in the snow. Crushing his cigarette, he mounted his winter bike and rode on. A bird flew down and circled him, then up and flew away. Yves smiled. "You are a bird now," he shouted as he pedalled towards the bridge.

*　　*　　*

Marlon and Andrea boarded the 2 o'clock Mega Bus headed for Toronto with one stop in Kingston. Marlon had been quiet in the waiting area of the station. Andrea respected his mood. After all, yesterday had been a very emotional day for everyone at the hall and online. Andrea learned so much from everyone. She had gotten a chance to speak to a few people and got to hear Marlon sing a few more times. She particularly enjoyed the chat she had with the two Caribbean ladies Dory and Shirley. She had been cornered for a small chat with the old French man who just wept about riding bikes and camping in the mountains. Andrea kept watch over Marlon, she was happy he stayed clear of the alcohol and just refreshed his tea most of the day.

When they took the bottom level seats on the bus, Andrea handed him a napkin-covered treat. Marlon unfolded the tissue to reveal two pieces of lemon loaf. He smiled and bit into one. Andrea remained quiet, hoping he would speak soon.

Marlon ate both pieces of cake then sipped from his canister of green tea.

"I..." he looked into the distance, wanting to say something, but found himself still afraid of his emotions.

"I thought I was right, I thought there was a right and a wrong. I lived my life holding such thoughts. I know wrong. I have been wrong, but on this I... I needed to be right the whole time. I was...wrong," he shrugged his shoulders. He continued in his mind, trying to understand, before the words were finally released.

"I thought God wouldn't give me half a woman, surely he thinks more of me than that. I deserve love and to be taken care of. I thought I did. So, when she came to me," he raised his voice slightly, "she offered me love. I saw it as a fraction a piece of what I or any man should have. Year after year had passed, and I figured out it's the long game. I expected her to get tired of a man who is willing to share her, and to come back to the man who loves her most. So every time I saw her, I was holding myself back. I wouldn't lay with her until she was mine alone. I let years pass, and all the while, I was holding this self-righteous position," he laughed before he continued. "As I was waiting, thinking about my eventual win, she was giving that slice of love to the French guy. She shared years of her life with a man who was happy to have her time, her love. That could have been me, but it wasn't. So, every time she saw me, oh she must have thought what a fool I was with my convictions and old-school ways."

'I am sure she didn't," Andrea offered

"Are you?" Marlon looked away as he remembered the conversation he had with Anton the day before.

After the toast, Ash and James headed out. Shirley and Pierre went back into the seating area to talk more. Darrin went to check on his Nan, who had decided to explain the wonders of childbirth to Sara.

Only Marlon and Anton remained in the small closed off area backstage. Anton was tired. This was one of the longest days he'd ever had.

"She would have loved this," Anton said, trying to find a smile for Marlon.

'I am sure, Charlene loved to be the centre of attention."

Both men chuckled. Anton filled his tiny cup with what was left in the bottle. He motioned to refill Marlon's glass, but Marlon declined. He had not drank a drop, even at the toast. When no one was looking he tossed his booze into a plant. A silent moment between them.

'So, this Pierre?" Marlon spoke first.

Anton nodded.

"Yeah, Pierre. He and Char had been lovers for a decade or so by the time I met her. He's a good man, she adored him," Anton explained.

Marlon didn't even know what question he wanted answered. Anton did. He just took a seat and started talking.

"Char didn't need anything from Pierre, nor he from her. He was an immigrant, from Cameroon, with little to no money. He worked two jobs, which kept him very busy. He sent money home to his family in Africa. He had no time for a full-time girlfriend, and no money for one. They enjoyed each other's company. She was very happy with the relationship."

"Sounds so simple," Marlon sat too.

Anton had always known of the struggles Charlene and Marlon had. He hoped Marlon would let go of some of his restraints, but every time they met, she came back shaking her head.

'She loved you," Anton said.

'How can she love all of us?" he challenged.

Anton took a moment. "Can only be you who decides how many people you can love. Charlene loved the people she wanted to love. She didn't hold feelings or affections hostage to serve a motive. She allowed her loved ones to come in when they wanted and to exit when they needed. She believed in the natural flow of love, letting things organically happen and not pushing. She gave the same energy she received. She called it a mirror. You kept her in a place with limitations. It was you that was limiting what you could have had. She was loved and happy. I hope that in all of this, you find happiness in that. Not pain in the fact that it wasn't just from you. You were loved as much as you allowed her to love you."

Anton was being called back to the large room. The private service was ending and soon throngs of Charlene's followers and friends would start piling in. He left Marlon alone with his thoughts and pain. Marlon found Andrea in the hall of photos soon after.

"I am ready to go now," his voice was soft.

"I took this," she said and smiled. "They said anyone can take whatever pics they want." Andrea held up a picture of Charlene and Marlon. They were very young. He was doing some form of dance move and she was laughing.

Marlon took the photo in his hand and looked at it for a long time.

Toronto

Cora placed a plate of scrambled eggs and toast in front of her brother. She was in a good mood, he thought. She spoke about the new baby coming into their lives the whole flight back to Toronto. She reminded him that by Christmas next year, Sara had promised a visit with the baby. "That is something to look forward to," she had said many times to Aaron.

The plate looked perfect. Soft yellow scrambled eggs, buttered toast and black tea.

"I am going to be a great Nana," she looked up at the painting of her and Charlene that Anton had given her.

Anton sipped his tea. He knew his sister was going to be okay now.

Boston

Leesa was nervous as she took a seat facing the window at her favourite café. She had a steamy cup of cappuccino in front of her and a powerful look in her eye.

She video called her ex, Samuel. She placed the phone in front of her so he could see her better.

"Hey babe, surprised you called. I really am hoping you are coming back. I miss you," he sounded so good, she just smiled.

"I need to talk to you about something," she started.

Sam listened through his head set as Leesa began explaining to him the benefits of a polyamorous lifestyle. She had done a ton of research and felt ready.

He couldn't believe what Leesa was saying. She had never shown any signs of moving in this direction. He had so many questions. He loved Leesa. He felt both scared and intrigued.

"Wow "was all he could say after she spoke.

"Boston is really progressive," he laughed.

Leesa shook her head. "I am not sure if it is or not, but I am deciding to be," She spoke clearly into her phone.

Montreal

Anton had finished cleaning the dishes and had taken the sheets off the spare bed. He started a load of laundry and waited for Shelly to return. Shelly had volunteered to drive Sara and Darrin to the airport. She would swing by the condo before heading home. He had promised to give her the painting she most loved. He took his time in the morning and wrapped it in the same cloth sheet he had seen Charlene wrap paintings up with in the past. It was going to be a lot of work packing up Charlene's things. But he would do it little by little with all the time in the world. Today a painting, tomorrow maybe her cycling gloves. Just small pieces at a time. She had lived such a huge life. It would take forever to remove all traces of her from the space. He was in no hurry.

Placing a record on the turntable, Anton relaxed on the small sofa letting his long legs hang over the end. The sun made its morning appearance into the large windows of his living room. He could see the faded image of Charlene dancing around the space like she always had.

*   *   *

The next morning, Montreal was covered in frost. All the windows in Pierre's apartment had a glossy glitter as the sun made them sparkle. Pierre opened his eyes to an exciting reality. Shirley was waking up, the sun hitting her face as she opened her eyes. She saw Pierre and blushed, as so many memories of the night before came rushing to her. The wine, the laughter, the take-away chicken dinner.

"Morning," she managed.

Pierre leaned in and kissed her on her bare shoulder as she used the sheet to hide herself. It was all so very distant from her comfort zone. Dory looked over at her newly purchased panties on the lamp. She wanted to laugh, but couldn't

"I didn't expect any of that," she said. She was both embarrassed and happy.

Pierre smiled. The evening had gone in a direction no one could have predicted. He remembered the wine and good company; he remembered his pain and taking a break.

'Moi aussie, me neither," he grinned. He was even more handsome when he smiled.

"Me neither!" Dory said, poking her head up from the covers on the other side of Pierre.

Shirley and Dory laughed, and Pierre joined in.

*   *   *

The airport was clamouring with people. Large groups were forming lines, ski equipment and large carry travel equipment were being pushed around. The Quebec police rode their bicycles through terminals. Darrin was being extremely protective of his wife and baby to be.

"I got this," He pulled both suitcases, not allowing her to assist in the carrying. After checking the bags, he sat Sara down next to the boarding gate and ran to the airport shop to get her a book and snacks for the flight. Sara enjoyed all the attention. It had been a week of people and emotions. Now it was just the tow of them flying back to their life. With a mystery novel and a bag of veggie chips in her hand, Sara handed the attractive woman her passport and boarded the plane.

Sara settled into her window seat. She was excited to be getting back to her life and making the changes that would need to be made. She was feeling quite good. It had been five days packed with so many emotions and thoughts. She still had not processed everything. She thought about Cora, the pretty little grandmother. She remembered the beautiful sound of Marlon's voice and the friendship she had forged with Shelly. *How can so much happen in less than a week?* she thought. She was now engaged and pregnant. She had met her new family. She would be in touch with Shelly and Anton regularly. She watched Darrin put their bags overhead before taking a seat beside her. He took her hand into his and held on tight.

The air hostess went through the emergency information as Darrin played with the ring absent-mindedly on Sara's finger.

"I am so glad you came with me," he expressed. "It was a lot, I know, but I couldn't have gotten through it..." he took in a deep breath.

Sara kissed him and sat back, ready for lift-off. The plane was moving very fast. Sara squeezed Darrin's hand again. She would probably not be able to fly again for some time. This meant that the next influx of family would be her family coming from Rotterdam. That would be a different kind of gathering altogether. She laughed to herself at the differences.

"Do you think your mother..." Sara began.

Sara looked over at Darrin, who was already sleeping as the airplane lifted off the ground.